"Ma'am, where do you hurt?"

Randy stared at the way her hands were gripping her stomach. "Are you in labor? Can you hear me?" He resisted the urge to push deeper inside the car. Forcing a tenuous position would put his victim at more risk. But a mother in danger—nothing got to him faster.

And this one mother...

Something about her seemed familiar, even if he couldn't put his finger on what. He scanned the parts of her body he could see, looking for anything he'd missed. Hair raised on the back of his neck.

His subconscious was trying to tell him something. What?

"Ah!" she cried, louder than before. "Help me..."

Randy's trained gaze cataloged each potential injury. It tracked up her torso and arms and shoulders, over the ebony hair framing the face that was finally uncovered.

A lover's face, not a stranger's.

"Oh, my God. Sam?"

Dear Reader,

My letter in *To Save a Family* promised readers a firefighter story was in the works. For several ATLANTA HEROES novels, I've been teasing everyone, including myself, with glimpses of the hunky Montgomery brothers. I fell in love with this trio of rescue workers, and so have many of the fans who've written me. Now, the wait is over!

The youngest of the brothers, firefighter Randy Montgomery, loves his siblings, and he loves saving lives. But when a secret baby and an ex-lover on the run from the mob drop into Randy's lap, his well-ordered world explodes. Sam Gianfraco is his match in every way, including her dark past and her distrust in happily-ever-afters. For the sake of their newborn daughter, can these soul mates follow their hearts and fight together, when life has taught them it's safer to battle alone?

While you read *The Firefighter's Secret Baby,* keep your eye out for future heroes. You'll love Charlie Montgomery for how hard he fights to protect his baby brother—you haven't seen the last of him, I promise. And there's another recurring character refusing to sit on the sidelines.... Bet you can guess who's lobbying the hardest to take the lead in my next Harlequin Superromance!

Until next time, dream big, love with your heart wide open, and love fearlessly.

Anna DeStefano

P.S. Let me know what you think of the ATLANTA HEROES stories at www.annawrites.com. And join the fun and fabulous giveaways at www.annawrites.com/blog!

The Firefighter's Secret Baby

Anna DeStefano

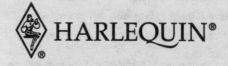

TORONTO • NEW YORK • LONDON
AMSTERDAM • PARIS • SYDNEY • HAMBURG
STOCKHOLM • ATHENS • TOKYO • MILAN • MADRID
PRAGUE • WARSAW • BUDAPEST • AUCKLAND

If you purchased this book without a cover you should be aware that this book is stolen property. It was reported as "unsold and destroyed" to the publisher, and neither the author nor the publisher has received any payment for this "stripped book."

Recycling programs
for this product may
not exist in your area.

ISBN-13: 978-0-373-71630-2

THE FIREFIGHTER'S SECRET BABY

Copyright © 2010 by Anna DeStefano.

All rights reserved. Except for use in any review, the reproduction or utilization of this work in whole or in part in any form by any electronic, mechanical or other means, now known or hereafter invented, including xerography, photocopying and recording, or in any information storage or retrieval system, is forbidden without the written permission of the publisher, Harlequin Enterprises Limited, 225 Duncan Mill Road, Don Mills, Ontario, Canada M3B 3K9.

This is a work of fiction. Names, characters, places and incidents are either the product of the author's imagination or are used fictitiously, and any resemblance to actual persons, living or dead, business establishments, events or locales is entirely coincidental.

This edition published by arrangement with Harlequin Books S.A.

For questions and comments about the quality of this book please contact us at Customer_eCare@Harlequin.ca.

® and TM are trademarks of the publisher. Trademarks indicated with ® are registered in the United States Patent and Trademark Office, the Canadian Trade Marks Office and in other countries.

www.eHarlequin.com

Printed in U.S.A.

ABOUT THE AUTHOR

Bestselling, award-winning author Anna DeStefano volunteers in the fields of grief recovery and crisis care. The rewards of walking with people through life's difficulties are never ending, as are the insights Anna has gained into what is most beautiful about the human spirit. She sees heroes everywhere she looks now. The top life lesson she's learned? Figure out what someone truly needs, become the one thing no one else could be for that person, and you'll be a hero, too!

For exciting news about her other Harlequin titles and her paranormal romantic suspense series, visit Anna at www.annawrites.com.

Books by Anna DeStefano

Don't miss any of our special offers. Write to us at the following address for information on our newest releases.

Harlequin Reader Service
U.S.: 3010 Walden Ave., P.O. Box 1325, Buffalo, NY 14269
Canadian: P.O. Box 609, Fort Erie, Ont. L2A 5X3

To those who stand and fight.

To those who run toward danger,
so others may be free.

To those who put all they are on the line.

To the heroes.

CHAPTER ONE

THUNDERSTORMS IN NOVEMBER?

Only in the south.

Sam peered through the greasy streaks her rental car's wipers were making of the rain. She squinted at her rearview mirror. Were those the same headlights as before? Was she just imagining the danger bearing down on her?

Yes, Sam.

It's been two years of constant fear, but you're imagining it all now.

A stabbing pain gripped her stomach. She forced her attention back to the road. Who cared who might be following her? She was going to careen into a guardrail if she didn't keep her eye on the road! She had to keep going. She had to get as far as she could before she tried to call her contact. Then everything would be okay. It had to be.

She was good at running, until the loneliness got too close. The hopelessness. Then she'd do something stupid. Something dangerous, because she needed to feel real for just a little while. She cradled her palm over the very real cramps in her belly.

Not anymore. Not after tonight. Once she made it through this, there would be no more risky chances. No more flirting with danger. Only playing it safe and protecting the lives that were depending on her.

She straightened her shoulders and tried to see through her rain-soaked windshield. Enough. What's done was done. Running was her only shot now. *Their* only shot. She refused to believe they couldn't make it.

"Whatever it takes," she said to her unborn child. "I won't let anything happen to you."

A film-noir-worthy bolt of lightning spotlighted where her latest risks had gotten her. The storm beat down on the car. Dark pines danced on either side of the interstate. Pain streaked through her body.

Her grip on the wheel tightened. Her tires lost traction for an eternal moment. Then they grabbed again.

"Focus, Sam," she hissed.

She hated the panic and fear. No matter what she did, she couldn't make them go away for good. But she *would* shove the darkness back. She wouldn't let the hopelessness win tonight. She just had to make it a little bit farther.

Past Atlanta. Out of the state. She had to get somewhere less on-the-map. Then she'd contact her federal handlers and find a way to trust them for a while longer. Long enough to testify and cut all ties with everyone and everything from her past—everything but her kid sister and her unborn child.

Headlights rushed from behind. A vehicle swerved

at breakneck speed, barely missing her back bumper. It passed on the shoulder. The truck careened in front of her, brake lights flashing. Its back end fishtailed. The 4x4's mud flaps sprayed a wave of water, blinding her.

Sam screamed and hit the brakes. Her tires spun and slid. Her car crossed into the next lane. She pulled at the wheel to avoid another vehicle.

Impact came with a horrible jolt. Her seat belt caught. Her head bashed into her window, cracking the safety glass. Dazed, she yanked the wheel again. The car swerved in protest. Then it skidded into the concrete median.

Scraping.

Dragging.

Her driver's door would be ripped away!

She fought for control. Blood trickled into her eyes. Pain ripped at her bulging stomach.

It's not going to end this way.

I'm not going to let it end this way…

Life became a slow motion nightmare. The truck that had cut her off barreled into a minivan. The van swerved in a deadly arc, crashing into her. Her rental car spun like a top while she banked the wheel and shoved the brake pedal to the floor.

More headlights. More rain. More vehicles crashing.

Lightning and thunder.

Terror.

Pain.

Then she was flipping, rolling, over and over. Glass shattering, metal shredding and crushing, while she wrapped her arms around her baby and prayed the seat belt would protect her daughter.

The windshield collapsed inward. Ice-cold rain soaked her. Her world shrank to the pinpoints of light spiraling behind her closed eyelids.

It was forever before anything made sense again. She realized the car was still rocking. Teetering. Her door had become the car's uncertain base.

Then she realized the pain was gone, too. The labor pains. She couldn't feel the baby moving, and her daughter was always moving these days. There was nothing left but the roaring in her ears. Her arms and legs were growing numb.

Shock.

She was going into shock.

"Please," she begged, praying for one more miracle. "Please, just give me one last chance...."

RANDY MONTGOMERY SCALED the pulverized wreck his team was securing. The air at the crash site vibrated with a frantic kind of calm while they prepared to crack the car with the Jaws of Life. The acrid smell of leaking fuel shimmered off everything Randy touched. His guys and several other teams responding to the multiple car pileup had doused the entire scene in fire retardant foam. But with this much petroleum in the mix, an errant spark could still set off a flash fire. It wasn't the worst scene Randy had triaged, but it would do.

And there had been many others. He'd certified in accident recovery in the first class that opened after 9/11, moving from an engine company to rescue because he'd thought that's where he could do the most good.

A faint, feminine groan whispered up from inside the vehicle.

He was point. His job was to triage and stabilize the victim for what promised to be a delicate extraction. Advanced life support would follow once his team had secured the vehicle.

"We have a live one," he called to his crew. "Someone position that spotlight over here."

Never lose a victim. It was Randy's mantra. He wasn't delusional enough to believe he had that kind of control. Still, he fought for every life with everything he had.

He reached through the slit that had once been the front passenger window—now the highest point of the rumpled vehicle. It would be his only view inside until a new one could be ripped open. He draped himself over the mangled mess of metal and fiberglass. There were razor-sharp edges to avoid. Possible weak spots. Stressing the wreck further could compromise the integrity of the safety cage. Randy let his instincts and years of experience guide him as he did his careful work of getting a visual on the victim.

Careful was his forte.

He stayed in control, no matter the crisis. *Ice* had been stenciled onto his helmet after he'd joined his first engine company, recognition of how hard he'd fought at every scene even as a newbie straight from the academy. His two older brothers, Chris and Charlie, whom he'd followed into fire and rescue, had given him the nickname. The moniker had stuck when Randy transferred to his rescue company.

It wasn't as if he didn't care about his victims. But as the go-to man on critical calls, emotion on the job wasn't a luxury he indulged in. And off the job… He was the son of a brutal father and an abused mother. Emotional entanglements weren't something he courted.

Levering as much of his body as he could through the sedan's passenger window, he took a deep breath and shoved his wandering thoughts away. He owed whomever was inside his total focus.

"What do you see, man?" The floodlights had been repositioned at a more direct angle, illuminating the safety cage that was manufactured into all modern vehicles.

"One occupant." He strained to see the still form huddled between the bent-back hood, what was left of the steering wheel, and the driver's door.

The body was covered in voluminous, blood-stained material. White cotton. Arms and legs, neither noticeably broken. The victim was lying on her side. Seat belt clipped into place and still attached. Sandals. One still on, the other lying close enough for Randy to reach.

"It's a woman." He cleared the delicate shoe from the field, along with whatever debris he could, transferring them down to waiting hands.

From the size of the body curled in on itself, the

victim appeared larger than average weight. Except *large* didn't jibe with the slender ankles and calves and arms and wrists he could see better as his eyes adjusted to the dimness. She groaned and shifted, rolling off her side. The car objected, rocking against the stabilization his men had added from the outside.

"Hold still, miss." Randy kept his voice reassuring. It was good that she could move. There wasn't as much blood as he'd originally thought. But— "You could have a spinal injury. There's glass and metal everywhere, and—"

She settled onto her back, still out of it, probably not hearing a word he said. But her protruding belly spoke loud and clear.

"Holy hell, she's pregnant!" He stretched his arm as far inside as he could, but he couldn't reach her. "Third trimester, if I had to guess."

In response to his raised voice, the victim's head gave an agitated jerk. Her features stayed hidden from him by a wealth of dark hair.

"Ma'am, where do you hurt?" He stared at the way her hands were gripping her stomach. "Are you in labor? Ma'am, can you hear me?"

Randy controlled the instinct to push deeper inside. Forcing a tenuous position would only put his victim at more risk. But a mother in danger—nothing got to Randy faster.

And this mother…

Something about her seemed familiar, even if he couldn't put his finger on what. He fought the urge to rip his way into the wreck. He forced himself to scan the parts of her body he could see, looking for anything he'd missed. Hair raised on the back of his neck.

His subconscious was trying to tell him something. What?

"Ah!" the woman cried out, louder than before. "Help me…"

Randy's trained gaze catalogued each potential injury. It tracked up her torso and arms and shoulders, over the ebony hair framing the face that was finally uncovered.

A lover's face, not a stranger's.

"Oh, my God. Sam?" Randy's focus jerked back to her swollen belly. He'd last seen her in his hotel-room bed in Savannah nine months ago…. "Oh, my God."

CHAPTER TWO

SAM TRIED TO RUN. She wouldn't give up. She had to keep fighting, even though a part of her knew that she couldn't move. There was something precious she had to save. A miracle she wouldn't let go of.

What was it,..

And there was that voice again. The one from her dreams.

She'd run from the voice before, back to the U.S. marshal in charge of her protection. She'd pulled herself together and regrouped. Hidden the memories of her lover and her reckless weekend in Savannah, so she could start over. Again. But the voice... It was so close now. Which meant so was the danger. The men chasing her. Had they found her?

"Sam?" the voice asked. "Can you hear me?"

No! her mind screamed.

Her name wasn't Sam anymore. *Sam* was being hunted. She couldn't be found. Not even in her dreams.

What was her name now?

"Robyn..." she insisted. "I'm Robyn Nobles."

Two years ago, Sam Gianfranco had left behind everything and everyone she knew. Even her baby sister. It had been the only way.

Except Sam had caved and called Gabriella that morning, before her security could tighten and she lost her chance. Her teenage sister had cried at the sound of Sam's voice. She'd begged Sam to come home. Too bad Gabby hadn't been the only one listening on the line.

They'd found Sam so quickly. One TV program. One phone call. One strange car parked outside her apartment...

Pain low in her belly jerked her away from the memories. Where was she? What had happened?

"My baby. Please, save my baby!"

"Sam?" the voice asked.

Her dreams had tormented her with that voice, night after night. She wanted Savannah back so badly. She wanted the precious life they'd created, more than she'd ever let herself want anything. She had to wake up! She had to keep fighting. Keep running.

"Get away from me," she whispered, terrified.

"Try to relax," the voice coaxed. "Trust me. We'll help your baby. We'll get you both out of this. Tell me where you hurt."

"Leave me alone!"

She tried to make her eyes open. To move.

Pain sliced through her. Reality came into blurry focus. She was lying on what used to be the side of her car, pinned against the shattered window. Totally helpless. Except she'd be damned if she'd just give up. Not while she could feel her daughter moving inside her again, fighting to live.

"You bastards," she gasped as another contraction took hold. "I won't let you hurt my baby. I'll kill you first."

Rage cleared her vision. But what she saw as she gazed up convinced her that she was still delirious. Because the face looking down at her belonged in her dream. Her baby's father was wearing a fire rescue uniform, not the metal band T-shirt he'd looked so sexy in on Savannah's River Street.

Was it real? His voice. Her terrifying need to trust him…

"Hold still, baby," he cautioned. "No one's going to hurt you. But you've gotta hold still, for your and the baby's sake."

"It—" The next contraction cut her in two. So did the concern in his gaze. "This isn't possible. You can't be—"

"It's me, sweetheart." He flashed that bad-boy grin that had weakened her knees. There was worry there, too, and a world of questions swirling behind his forced confidence. "You sure know how to get a country boy's attention."

Then he winked, God help her. A surreal giggle escaped her chest. A croaking cough followed. The kind of cough that old people made when they only had a few breaths left.

Sam let the memories flood back. They were stronger than reality. Closer. Memories that reminded her how much she'd needed him over the last nine months. Memories of a strong, dark-haired man with deep brown eyes and a surprisingly gentle touch. Of how his playfulness had given way to a passion she couldn't resist. Just like she couldn't stop herself from gazing up at him now and clinging to the miracle of him being there.

"Sam?" that voice from her dreams said.

"Randy?"

"You may be hurt badly, baby." The car shifted around her. Then the magic of his touch was smoothing across her cheek, down to the pulse beating a tantrum at the base of her throat. "You have to hold still until we can free you from this mess. Stay with me, Sam. Do you hear me? Sam? Damn it, answer me!"

"I… I'm here. My stomach… Ah!" She tried to draw her legs up against the next wave of cramps, but she couldn't pull them close enough. "It hurts."

"I know. You have to hold still until we can stabilize your entire body." He pulled away. Yelled something toward the footsteps she could hear outside the car. Then his handsome face reappeared above her. His helmet was gone. His hair was tousled and matted with sweat, even though Sam was freezing from the cold night air. He inched his body back inside, a little closer this time. "Does anything else hurt besides your belly? Does it feel like your water's broken?"

"How…"

How could Randy be there, exactly when she and her baby needed him most?

He'd asked her a question.

Where did it hurt?

Actually…

"I… I can't feel much of anything again." The

next contraction was weaker than the last. "The baby's not moving as much…"

"Just hang tight," he said. "We'll get you out of there."

Despite his assurances, Randy's voice had tightened. He was pushing even further into the unstable wreck.

"Help me," she begged.

"What the hell are you doing, Montgomery?" someone demanded. "You trying to bring the whole damn thing down on top of us! We don't have this mess secured. Back off!"

And that's when Sam saw the truth in Randy's eyes.

"I'm dying, aren't I?" she asked. "Because I didn't wait for my security. Because I panicked. They don't know where I am, and…and it's too late, anyway. But the baby—"

"Are you kidding me?" Randy flashed his killer grin again. "There's no such thing as too late. Not on my watch. Losing you would ruin my rep. You're not going to do that to me, are you? Keep talking until my guys can get me all the way in there, okay? Stay with me, Sam. Talk to me about something good. Tell me… Tell me about your baby."

Her baby. The only reality that mattered now.

"It's not just my baby…" Sam closed her eyes. The concern on Randy's face, the shredded mess she'd made of the car. The memory of Gabby's voice over the phone. It was all twisting together now. Pulling Sam in a million directions. Further away from Randy.

No!

Not until he promised.

She forced her eyes open. She had to see his face. She had to tell him.

"No matter what happens to me, take the baby," she whispered. "Promise me you'll protect her. Don't let them hurt her…."

"Let who hurt her?"

Randy's frown, the protectiveness behind his bewildered tone, pierced Sam's heart.

"Who are you running from?" he asked over the growing racket outside the car. "Is that why you weren't there when I woke up that morning? Tell me who's got you so scared, Sam. Let me help you."

This wasn't about her. She had to make him understand.

"No! Our daughter." Sam shook her head. She could hardly see him now. "This baby…she's yours. Don't tell anyone that you know. Don't trust anyone. But you have to protect her, Randy. Promise me… Don't let him destroy our baby, too…."

"CAREFUL!" There was nothing about being on the outside of an extraction, looking in, that Randy had ever liked. But waiting was his job, once he'd scouted the wreck and his team was in place. Getting out of the way and letting the other guys work was the best thing for a victim. Except this was no ordinary victim his men were fighting to free.

The last time—the only other time—he'd seen Sam, they'd slept together. Except what they'd shared went deeper. From the second he'd first seen her, he'd sensed she was different. Special. Now, nearly nine months later, she was pregnant and fighting for her life at an accident scene that was at the moment beyond Randy's control.

The storm raged on around them. Rain was showing no sign of letting up. The hydraulic drive of the Jaws of Life made a deafening sound as it did its dirty work. The cutters had already sliced through the crumpled roof and the car's dash. The guys were readying the spreader and ram, techniques for opening and lifting the interior of a vehicle enough to clear space for EMTs to get in. That was, if they didn't bring the whole mess down on top of the woman who'd said she was carrying Randy's baby.

The equipment started up again and the entire car shook. Randy felt the next crash in his bones.

"Careful!" he snarled.

"Easy, man," Donaldson said beside him. He wiped his sleeve over his eyes to clear the rain splattering under the bridge of his helmet. "They got it under control."

"Yeah, I know."

Randy's guys rocked. Each team member trusting the other was the key to saving a victim. Any delay he caused by distracting the other men could be the extra time the medical professionals needed to preserve life.

Except this was Sam.

Randy had to get to her. He had to talk to her. Ask her a million questions, especially about the baby.

She's yours, too. Don't tell anyone that you know. Don't trust anyone… Protect her. Promise me.

What the hell had she meant, *Don't let him destroy our baby, too?*

An Atlanta police officer trudged through the storm and toward the impending temper tantrum Randy was going to have if Sam wasn't free in the next five minutes.

"Do we have an ID yet?" the officer asked.

APD's first priority was to secure the scene and reroute traffic. Only then did they worry about who was involved in the accident itself.

"No," Randy yelled over his team's work. Had Sam really meant not to trust anyone? Even the police? "I didn't get to anything personal while I triaged her. She's delirious. Not making much sense. I'd recommend investigating the possibility she was run off the road. Sounds like there was another car involved."

Delirious or not, Sam had said someone was trying to kill her.

"Yeah." The officer motioned behind him with his thumb. "That federal marshal over there suggested the same thing. But we don't have enough details from witnesses yet to classify it a hit-and-run. Did she say—"

"She's out of her mind in pain, and prematurely delivering her baby!" Randy caught Donaldson's narrowed glance at his outburst. He sighed and gave the officer his full attention. "You're going to have to wait until… Wait. What federal marshal?"

A tall man had followed the officer. His dark business suit was unwrinkled and spotless, despite the water the storm was dumping on him. Everyone else at the scene looked like drowned rats.

"I need whatever information you can give me about what happened here," he said. "Tell me what the victim in that car has said to the first responders."

"You need to step back, sir." Randy indicated to a spot well away from the scene. His raised eyebrow asked the APD officer what was going on.

"Yeah." APD crossed his arms. "That's what I was trying to tell him. But—"

"I'm a deputy federal marshal." The man pulled a wallet from his coat and flashed a badge. "The name's Max Dean."

"Dean?" Seriously? It sounded like something out of a western. "Well, Marshal Dean. Your information is currently trapped inside a few tons of scrap metal. You're going to have to step back and—"

"I assure you I have the authority to conduct whatever investigation is necessary," the man said.

And Randy was going to keep everyone the hell away from Sam, until she was safe and could explain what was going on.

"Your federal authority is real impressive and all." Randy produced his slowest southern-boy smile. "But the security of this scene and everyone here is my call until EMT has my victim stabilized. You're going to wait, *sir*. For your own safety, of course."

"We're in!" Gibson shouted from the wreck.

Randy's crew was already disengaging their tools. They'd have the EMT team in place in under sixty seconds.

"I need to get in there." Dean tried to shoulder his way closer.

Randy braced a forearm against the marshal's chest.

"Let my team work." Randy curbed his own impulse to rush to Sam. "All it takes is one slip of our equipment. One miscalculated move. The victim was unconscious when I climbed down. Before that, she was talking nonsense. There's nothing for you to do here, unless you're trying to put her life in even more danger."

Randy studied the marshal's reaction. There was nothing to see but the man's growing irritation. Whatever Dean was doing there, he didn't give a shit about Sam.

A female EMT eased into the wreck. Her partner hunkered down and began feeding her equipment and supplies.

"You spoke with the driver?" Dean wanted to know.

Randy didn't answer. He didn't breathe. He narrowed his attention to what was happening in the car.

"What exactly did you two discuss?" the marshal pressed. "I need to be made aware of everything that's happened. Your victim is a principal in one of my operations."

Randy grabbed the man by his suit's rain-soaked lapels, losing patience with every out-of-control thing swirling around him.

"All you need to be aware of, is that your *principal* is most likely about to lose her baby, if not her own life!"

CHAPTER THREE

SAM SURFACED from the nightmare. She could hear Max's voice. He was nearby. Separate from the fuzziness of her thoughts. What was Max doing in her bedroom? Why couldn't she get her eyes to open?

Other voices were clamoring around her. Above her. Someone reported on her condition. Very official. Something pinched her arm, then her hand. There was talk about IVs and leads. Beyond it all, Sam could still hear her federal marshal.

Max sounded furious. But whatever was wrong, he would take care of it. And something was wrong. That was the one thing she was sure of. What had she done this time?

Max was shouting at someone....

Randy?

Why was she dreaming about the federal marshal in charge of her protection arguing with a long-ago voice she refused to let herself think about anymore?

Unless...

Sam's belly cramped. Rain flooded over her. A storm raged around her, beyond her, beating against her face.

She hurt.

Everywhere.

"Ah!" she gasped, reality racing back.

The vehicle chasing her… The accident! Randy being there when he shouldn't have been, his deep voice and the concern in his eyes and his warm touch. It was real. It was all real.

She'd told him to protect the baby. *Their* baby. She'd told him too much. She hadn't told him enough. Now Max was there, and the two of them were arguing. What had she done?

She tried to fight the pain and the weight pressing down on her body.

Move!

Warn Randy!

"The APD is under my authority at this scene," Max shouted. "You can't keep me from interviewing her. And you wouldn't want to if you knew what was at stake."

"Then fill me in," Randy demanded. "Otherwise, medical attention is all she's receiving. The hell with your interview.

"Isolate her from all but essential personnel," Max insisted.

An incredulous laugh followed.

"Okay," he said. "Which of my team or the cops or the EMTs do you consider unessential?"

"I can have you restrained, Lieutenant, if that's what it takes to—"

"Try it. You're not *isolating* this victim from me, Marshal Dean. Not until I—"

"You got her out alive." Max's voice held an edge Sam had never heard before. Or maybe it was the buzzing in her ears that was growing louder, washing over every word until she had to strain to hear. "Job well done. Now get the hell out of the way and let me do mine. Before…"

"Before what?" Randy wanted to know. "What the hell is going on?"

"We need to transport her," another voice said. Something gripped Sam's arm. Tight. Tighter. "Her pressure's bottoming out. If we don't get her and the baby to the hospital…"

The pain and the fear and Sam's need to tell Randy to listen to Max and get out before the danger got too close—it was all fading, along with the cramping in her belly that was her baby fighting for her life. The dream was there again, reaching for her.

The one where her daughter would be okay no matter what happened to Sam. Because Randy was there. He was smiling. Promising her he'd protect their child. Inside the dream, Sam could believe in promises and happily-ever-afters.

"My baby…" she finally managed to say out loud.

His touch stroked down her hair. She felt him lean closer. "You and the baby are going to be okay."

"Protect our daughter, no matter what," she whispered to him. She'd spent nine months telling herself she had to let the ridiculous fantasy of being with Randy go. Now, it felt as if he was the only thing standing between their child and the danger Sam had brought into their lives. "Never should have happened… All my fault. But you have to—"

"Everything's fine, Robyn," Max reassured her. He was closer, too. "We're going to get you—"

"Robyn?" Randy asked.

"Robyn Nobles. That's your victim's name." There was a silent pause. "Or is there something else you need to tell me?"

"I don't need to tell you a damn thing!"

"Please stop," she begged them both. "It doesn't matter anymore."

She fumbled for Randy's hand. She could barely feel it in her own.

Maybe it was the weakness stealing through her. Maybe it was having Randy there. But it finally felt safe. She could let the fear and the fight go. There was nothing else to do. There was only this moment. It had all come down to this. Even if she didn't make it, there would be someone there for her daughter.

"Promise me." She squeezed Randy's hand. "Take care of our baby…."

"WHAT DO YOU MEAN, it's too early to tell?" Randy had been badgering Atlanta Memorial's top pediatric nurse for ten minutes.

He was being an ass, but his head was too full of pointless questions. He needed answers, and Kate Rhodes had been a family friend for years. As soon as she'd gotten wind that he'd ridden along with Sam's ambulance and staked out the O.R. waiting room, she'd found him and stayed glued to his side, no matter how much he growled.

"Emma will be here soon," she said. "I'm sure she headed over the second you called her. Once she's here, I'll find your victim and get more information. Her injuries looked surprisingly minor, considering what I've heard about the accident. But her pregnancy puts her at greater risk for complications—"

"I don't need you to hold my hand until my big sister gets here. I need to know what's going on. Go—"

"Not while you're making the kind of scene that's going to get you tossed off this floor."

Kate dragged him to a chair. She was a tall woman, but Randy still towered over her. She got him to sit, regardless, then settled beside him. The room was silent around them. They were alone, at least for the moment. He was still soaking wet and filthy from the scene. And Kate was right—he was punch drunk, reeling from everything that had happened.

"Why are you so hung up on this victim?" she asked. "You're usually thrilled to be the hero who walks off into the sunset. Not that anyone you've saved has ever complained. But it's not like you to let the job get personal, Randy."

No, no one complained. And no one ever got close enough to mess with the calm Randy had carved out for his life. That's how he wanted his career. That's how he wanted his relationships outside his family. Except for the chaos his brothers and sister supplied in a steady stream, Randy just wanted peace. A peace that had been unsettled for months by his bizarre attachment to a woman he barely knew. And now...

Don't let him destroy our baby, too...

Your victim is a principal in one of my operations....

"Who is she?" Kate asked.

Randy managed a careless shrug. "A pregnant twentysomething who's banged up and giving birth."

"Yeah. I could have read that off the EMT's report. But who's she to you? Where are her people? It's been hours since the accident. You're the only one here waiting to see what happens."

Randy nodded, even though he was certain Federal Marshal Max Dean was ruthlessly asserting his authority somewhere nearby. Which only added to Randy's determination to get some answers. He had no reason to believe that Sam's child was really his, or to feel responsible for their well-being. But there had been cold deliberation in Dean's eyes. Randy couldn't shake the unreasonable compulsion to protect Sam from the man and whatever had her so terrified.

Reason was how his world of fire and rescue worked. Except fear had taken control when he'd surprised his team and insisted on riding in Sam's ambulance. Fear had kept him pacing at Atlanta Memorial ever since.

"I have no idea who she is," he finally said. "But... I have to know she and her baby are okay."

Kate nodded slowly.

"Martin said APD alerts have gone out, trying to find hits for her ID and description." Kate's hulking brother taught at the police academy, which gave him a lot of contacts in the Atlanta Police Department. "I suppose it's possible no one knows she's missing yet."

"It's also possible the ID we found in her purse is a dead end, and we're not meant to find out where she and her baby belong."

"Is that why you're calling her Sam when her license says her name is Robyn?"

"Something like that." *Don't tell anyone you know....*

"You don't think this was just another accident, do you?"

"Witnesses at the scene said someone hit a minivan, sending it skidding into her car. It sounds like the truck that caused the pileup had been dogging Sam for miles."

"And how, exactly, do you know this *Sam?* Why don't you want me using any other name but Robyn Nobles with the staff?"

Kate's perfectly logical questions hung in the air, waiting for perfectly logical answers.

"Got a dollar?" Randy asked.

Kate fished into the pocket of her scrubs and handed a bill over. Randy headed for the hall and the dilapidated vending machine that had already denied him Yoo-hoo twice. Ignoring his friend, who walked at his side, Randy inserted the money into the machine.

Wrrr.

Grind.

It spat the bill back out at him.

"Damn it!" He pounded the side of the contraption with a clenched fist and inserted the dollar again.

"So, your plan is to make Herbie pay, " Kate said, "because you can't smack around anyone else?"

"Herbie?" The bill flew back out of the slot and drifted to Randy's feet. He growled and bent over to pick it up.

"This old wreck picks and chooses who it wants to bestow its bounty on. It's not mercenary. Herbie always refunds your money if he's not feeling the love. But he's fickle. Reacts badly to stress. And from the looks of you, *I* kind of feel bad for whatever soda you get your hands on. You'll crush it to oblivion when you're done. You can understand why Herbie would feel protective."

Randy stared at her. Never-ending overtime on the pediatric ward and dressing daily in cartoon scrubs had finally shredded her sanity. He wadded her dollar into a ball. Kate chuckled. He threw the money to the floor and stomped away.

He was furious. Deadly furious—at himself, not a tyrannical drink machine. He didn't know anything about the woman his team had extracted. Not her mind. Her fears. Her secrets. All he knew was the instinct to keep her, now that he had her back. The memory of Sam's contented sighs in that hotel room in Savannah had been messing with his head for months. Was that really all this was—him still being hung up on a one-night stand?

He might be a shallow sonovabitch when it came to relationships, but him losing it was about more than not being with another woman since St. Patrick's Day. Seeing Sam again had stirred up more than a physical itch he needed to scratch. He was terrified for her and her unborn baby. It had been a lifetime since any emotion had gotten this close.

The elevator by the soda machine dinged. Randy's sister emerged.

"Hey, Em," Kate said.

Emma stepped onto the floor, stalled beside Herbie and pulled a wrinkled bill from her purse. She fed the machine, scooped up the can that was agreeably provided, collected her change and marched down the hall toward them. Her expression was worried, but her determined stride said *I've got this covered.*

Classic Emma.

She'd had everything covered for as far back as Randy would let his memory go. She reached his side and held out the can.

"You must be needing a chocolate fix something awful by now," she said.

Kate hugged her, then she and her pink scrubs with yellow ducks floating all over them were heading down the hall.

"I'll let you know when there's an update on our patients," she said over her shoulder.

"Patients?" Emma asked while Randy sat in one of the lounge's chairs and snapped open his drink. She joined him. "You said you knew a woman in the accident. That you might need Rick's help with information about her. Was there someone else in her car?"

Randy downed half the Yoo-hoo and let its coolness take the edge off the drive to go hand-to-hand with Herbie.

"There's a baby." He tunneled his free hand through his hair. "The victim is pregnant. Very pregnant. *It's only a matter of hours* pregnant. No one's saying anything about either of their conditions yet."

"And?" Emma had on her lawyer's face. The one that revealed nothing about what she was feeling, while she listened to absolutely everything that was being said.

"And it sounds like Sam and the baby were in trouble a long time before the MVA," he added. The kind of trouble that Emma's APD detective husband could look into.

"And?" Emma asked again.

"And I owe it to her to—"

"*Owe* it to her?" Emma slipped her hand into his, like she had when he was a little boy and their world had fallen apart. "Randy, this woman. How do you—"

"We…met, on my trip down to Savannah in March."

Emma watched him drain the last of his drink. When he still didn't say anything else, she headed back to the vending machine and beguiled another can out of the beast. She returned to Randy's side, her eyes narrowing.

Her mind had always been able to sift through facts faster than should be legal.

"So, you met this woman the weekend you and

Chris and Charlie and some of the guys headed south to blow off steam," she said. "Only you came back more uptight than ever. You've been impossible to deal with since, the few times any of us have seen you off the job. All because of some hook-up you haven't wanted to talk about. And now she's here…and she's *very* pregnant?"

"Yeah." Randy took the fresh Yoo-hoo. He handed over his empty can, which he didn't remember crushing. The thing was little more than a ball of aluminum now. "That weekend… It was strange. We were both looking for something easy and fun. It shouldn't have meant anything more. Except it did, somehow. Being with her was…different. There was a connection. At least, I thought there was. But when I woke up the next morning, Sam had bolted. I figured I'd never see her again and tried to tell myself it was a good thing."

"And now that you have seen her again?"

Randy curled both hands around his drink.

"She's in trouble, Em. I'm sure of it. Nothing she was saying at the scene made any sense. I think she may have been in trouble when I met her in March, too. Maybe that's what stuck with me all this time— what I couldn't let go of."

"You do have a weakness for saving people." Emma nudged his shoulder with hers, only half kidding. "My little brother, the hero."

Her biggest worry for him—for Randy and both his brothers—was how much of themselves they buried in their jobs. For Randy and Charlie and Chris, navigating relationships was the impossible thing—not walking into blazing infernos for a living. So far, Em had been the only one who'd been able to carve out a life with someone.

"If Sam wanted my help," Randy reasoned out loud, "she wouldn't have run that morning."

"I don't know about that. I almost torched what I had with Rick, before I learned how to stop shoving him away."

"That was different."

Emma had always been different.

"Yeah," she agreed. "I wasn't pregnant with Rick's baby when he gave me the space to realize I couldn't live without him. If I'd been carrying his child, he wouldn't have let me out of his sight, whether I wanted to be saved or not."

"I don't know what this woman wants. I don't have the first clue what's going on."

It wasn't an admission anyone who knew Randy was used to hearing. His sister's eyebrows disappeared beneath her honey-colored bangs. But she didn't push. Her silence was an open invitation to trust her with more, whenever he was ready.

And Randy did trust her. There was nothing his family wouldn't do for him. Whatever secret Sam was keeping, even if the danger she'd been rambling about was real, Randy's brothers and sister would be his safety net.

"She said someone was after her," he admitted. "That whoever it was would be back, and she and the baby were in danger. I don't know how much of it is true, or even if the child is mine. But she was terrified. Then a federal marshal showed up on the scene...."

Emma nodded. Her lawyer's face was back, but she was holding Randy's hand again.

"And you need to know what about Sam's situation is real," she said. "So you'll know where you stand once she's stable enough for you to ask about the rest."

The rest.

Sam and the baby and what the hell they meant to Randy...

"I need Rick's help, Em. Your husband's a bulldog. He knows exactly how to bend the rules without breaking anything important. He's served as APD liaison on task forces with God knows how many federal agencies. He has to have a few favors to call in. I need to know everything he can dig up on this woman, her federal handler and whoever she's running from."

CHAPTER FOUR

"EXCUSES ARE USELESS TO ME."

Luca Gianfranco smoothed a hand down the tie that, along with his private Gulfstream jet, was ruinously expensive but worth every dime he'd spent. In his world, money was power. It intimidated the people he needed kept in place, and wooed the ones he wanted closer.

Know who you can trust, and deal firmly with the ones you can't.

It had been the wisest advice Luca's father had ever given him.

"I guarantee she couldn't have survived that accident," the head of Luca's southeastern operations insisted over their cell link.

"Really? Because it occurs to me that a guarantee would have been you watching her take her last breath."

"Fire and rescue was there in under ten minutes. We couldn't have—"

"You chose to make a public spectacle out of your responsibility, then you didn't finish the job. Almost as if you didn't want the same outcome I do, and you didn't want me to have another chance once you failed."

"I did what you asked," said the voice of a man Luca had been sure could be trusted. It wasn't the first time he'd been wrong about family. "You wanted the world to know you aren't weak. No matter what you have to do. No one who hears about how you took Sam out will doubt—"

"But I haven't taken her out. She was rushed to the hospital. She's been in emergency surgery for hours." Luca took a deep breath, resisting the wave of familiarity that came with thinking of her as *Sam*. She was a loose end. A challenge to his control that would be his death warrant if he didn't eliminate her.

There was a long pause.

Something crashed on the other side of the line.

"She's alive?" the gruff voice said.

"I'm assured she's in bad shape, but alive. That's all the details I can get. My source won't risk attracting suspicion by asking too many questions. But that's a risk I'm confident you'd be happy to take, to make up for your failure."

"But even if I can get someone to—"

"Get your ass over there. I want a detailed report before morning. Then I'll tell you exactly what I want done to end this. The trial's less than a month away. My Vancouver associates are nervous. I'm on my way to reassure them that I've isolated the leak, that there's no way I'll be indicted, and that their investment is secure. You either take care of this for me, or you become part of the collateral damage you caused."

Luca slapped his phone shut. The flight attendant

bringing him cappuccino flinched as she set the cup down. He caught her hand before she could draw away.

"Share some of this with me?" It wasn't a request.

She sat. Her smile was beautiful, if not completely genuine. She didn't resist as Luca's fingers threaded through hers. He lifted the cup of steaming coffee with his free hand, offering it to her as if it were a precious jewel. Hesitating, she took a sip and licked foam from her upper lip.

Sam had once craved private time with him. She'd needed companionship and a sense of belonging so badly. She'd been his shadow, until she betrayed him.

Luca's hand tightened around the attendant's, becoming a crushing vise. A squeak of pain escaped as he leaned forward, staring into her blue eyes. The same color as Sam's.

"No one leaves my family," he whispered to the attendant.

His mind raced with his plans to expand his West Coast operations into Vancouver. Everything was riding on him neutralizing this ridiculous grand jury mess. His fist clenched tighter. A bone snapped in the petite blonde's hand. She cried out. The thrill of it swamped the rush of unfamiliar anxiety that had momentarily taken hold.

"No one challenges me," he explained, his voice gentle. "Understand?"

The flight attendant nodded frantically, her eyes glazing. Pain. Fear. It was the same broken expression that had been on Sam's face the night she'd run from him and their world. He wanted to see fear in her eyes again, just once more before she died. Fear of him, while he took away the life she had no right to live without his permission.

"You'd never betray me." He yanked the attendant closer, until their lips brushed. "Would you?"

"YOU HAVE TO DO THIS," Charlie Montgomery insisted, begging for help from a man he'd once threatened to kill with his bare hands.

His family's relationship with their sister's husband had come a long way since he and Chris and Randy had tried to beat the crap out of Rick Downing on Emma's front lawn.

"I've never seen Randy this way," he pressed when Rick didn't respond. "Not even when we were kids. Not even when…"

"I understand." Emma's APD hero husband sounded both sympathetic and annoyingly professional. "But there's no way—"

"There is, too, a goddamned way!" Charlie thundered.

This was Charlie's baby brother they were talking about. Helping Randy through the first crisis any of them had seen get to him since they were kids—that was the *only* way. Except Rick didn't know Randy like the rest of them. He couldn't know how out of character Randy asking for Emma's help had been— then asking Charlie to wade into the situation when Emma had come up empty.

"When it was your best friend's ass on the line," Charlie said, "you pushed and shoved until you were right in the middle of an FBI sting Alexa Vegas got herself in. When my sister told you to butt out of her life and turned my brothers and me loose on you, you took us all on to stay by her side. You put your job on the line to help her and get her to believe in you. But my brother's problems aren't important enough to risk your neck for, is that it?"

Rick was the big gun Charlie and his family needed. He'd married their sister last year, and they'd all accepted him, regardless of the bad blood between their families. It was time for the man to prove he knew what family meant.

Rick folded his arms across his chest. The guy was talking himself out of letting those meaty fists of his fly—a diversion Charlie would have welcomed at the moment.

Damn, he hated being back at Atlanta Memorial. Even though he didn't personally know the patient they were all waiting around to hear news about, the place gave him the creeps. It hadn't been that long ago that Emma had been the one clinging to life, after a courthouse shooting left her bleeding in Rick's arms.

"Say whatever you got to say," Charlie challenged. "I have got no feelings for you to hurt. And I got no problem taking you on right here and now, if you don't care how much it's hurting Emma to watch Randy fall apart over a stranger while there's something you can do to help him."

"There's nothing I wouldn't do for my wife, as long as my actions don't make the situation worse. And from what I've heard, that's exactly what would happen if I started throwing my weight around digging for answers. Martin Rhodes already got nowhere trying to find information on this Robyn Nobles woman."

"Making things worse for your cushy career, you mean."

"No, you asshole." Downing slid his hands into his filthy jeans pockets. The guy had come to the hospital straight from work. Being a detective meant he wore whatever earned him the street cred he needed. "Worse for Emma, when my questions put someone her brother cares about at even more risk."

Rick had clearly done a bit of digging already.

"What have you heard?" Charlie asked.

"Not much." Rick scanned the empty waiting area. Chris had dragged Emma downstairs for coffee. Lord knew where Randy was prowling while he waited like a caged lion for an update about this woman and her baby. "Except that the guys' weekend you took down the coast may have landed Randy in the middle of a whole lot of shit he was never supposed to be involved in."

"Well, he's involved now. At least enough to ask his own questions if I can't get them for him through safer channels. Think about what that will do, if things are as dicey as you say. He's attached to this woman, whether the rest of us understand it or not. I've never seen him like this. Chris or Emma neither. Randy's all about logic and reason and keeping things simple. But he's neck deep in whatever this is and not looking for a way out. All for a woman he hasn't spent more than a few hours with. I don't see him stopping until he has some answers, do you?"

A wave of understanding passed between them. Randy might work nonstop and party hard and all the other things that guaranteed his personal life stayed superficial and uncomplicated. But nothing stopped him when it came to keeping the people he really cared about safe. And this accident victim had Randy caring like she was family—in the midst of a situation that sounded more unstable by the second.

"Get my brother whatever information you can," Charlie insisted. "Whatever it's going to take to keep him and this woman safe."

"Randy should back off. Now."

"That's not going to happen."

"Not even if pushing might be the worst thing he could do for the lady in question?"

"He'll never believe that, not after she begged him for his help."

"She was delirious. Injured. Giving birth."

"And she reached out for my brother, after nine months of the rest of us having to deal with him sulking because he couldn't see her again. She told him she was in so much trouble he shouldn't say anything to anyone, but he's trusting my family. Now we're trusting you. He needs your help, Rick. We all do."

Downing blinked at the closest to begging Charlie had ever come. Then he nodded.

Simple.

Direct.

Rick was all-in, the same way he'd been when it had been Emma's well-being on the line.

"All right," Rick said. "I'll get you everything I can. Just don't expect to like it. And don't expect my information to make whatever Randy's next decision has to be any easier."

CHAPTER FIVE

SAM COULD HEAR, but she couldn't feel. She could remember, but only what was far away. What was closer, what was happening around her, made no sense.

All that made sense was that she had to be sure. She had to make him understand. He had to keep their baby safe.

"You have to believe me!" she whimpered.

Whimpered?

The woman who'd ditched Luca Gianfranco and stayed ditched for nearly two years didn't whimper. About anything.

"Try to relax," a soothing feminine voice said.

Then the voice belonged to a nurse wearing pink clothes that were covered in ducks.

Not the *him* Sam had been begging.

Not Randy.

Had he only been part of a dream? Everything was so muddled. Sam could remember feeling safe, because Randy had been there. Even though Luca would keep coming for her...

"Your baby will be here soon," the nurse said. "The doctors want to deliver her without a C-section.

They're bringing you around enough to push, but there will be no pain."

"My baby…"

The room swam into sharper focus. She was in an O.R. Her nurse was wearing a surgical mask. Other people moved around her.

Terrifying flashes of the accident sliced through her pounding head. She clenched her fingers against her cramping stomach.

"My baby!" It had all been real. The accident. Randy. Going into labor. Was it too late? "Is she—"

"Your little girl's fine." The pretty nurse smiled. "We did an ultrasound. She's in distress, but as long as we deliver her soon, she'll be fine. Your condition is stabilized. You'll need a sling to protect your shoulder for a while, but somehow nothing was broken. Your head injury is minor. There are stitches, and we'll have to monitor your concussion for a few days. But the seat belt seems to have saved you from the worst of it."

But not her baby.

Sam wasn't due for another two weeks.

Everything that had happened swirled through Sam like bolts of sizzling lightning that couldn't hurt her, because they weren't quite real. All that felt real was the man she'd been dreaming about for close to a year. A stranger who'd left her with a piece of himself. A miracle. A promise that there would be a tomorrow.

"Randy's baby…" Sam whispered.

A moment of shock crossed the other woman's face.

"Do you know him?" Sam asked, grappling to

remember what his response had been to her revelation that he had a child on the way. A daughter who was in danger. But there was nothing there—no memory to reassure her. "You have to make him believe me. You have to tell him. Luca… Don't let Luca hurt our baby…."

"…she's hemorrhaging…"

"The baby's heart rate…"

"Save her," Sam begged. "Tell Randy he has to…"

"…can tell him yourself," the nurse was saying. "We'll take good care…your baby and you…"

"…fully effaced… This baby's delivering now!"

The nurse was lifting Sam's shoulders. She'd been right, there was no pain. Only the need to push so her daughter—Randy's daughter—could be born. The nurse supported Sam's back. Everything faded but the realization that the baby was coming. It still wasn't safe. Luca couldn't know there was a child. But—

Voices told her to push.

To push again.

Pressure.

More pressure.

Then, finally, relief, followed by a wave of loneliness no drug could numb.

"She's beautiful." The nurse eased Sam back.

"Is she…" Sam was so tired, but she had to know. "Is she okay? She…she isn't crying…"

"Let the doctors take care of her," the nurse said.

"You're going to sleep again," a male voice added.

"No! I want to see her. Just once…" Sam fought the touch restraining her.

"You'll see her when you wake up," the nurse reassured her. "You and your daughter are safe. Rest…"

"You don't understand…" What if she didn't wake up quickly enough? What if she didn't wake up at all? Someone had to make Randy understand.

They'd be back.

Luca's men.

They'd come for her. Luca would come for her baby, and Sam didn't trust the feds to protect her daughter. A child wouldn't be their priority. Sam's testimony was all they cared about.

Where was Randy?

Randy had to know. He had to keep their daughter out of Luca's clutches. And he would. Sam had sensed it the morning she'd woken in his hotel room in Savannah. Randy was the kind of man who'd stop at nothing to protect someone he cared about. She'd run from the temptation of wanting to be cared for that completely.

Now she was reaching for the dream, needing it to be real while the world faded.

"Tell Randy he has to protect our baby." She fought the pull of the drugs. "Tell him… I'm so sorry I've done this to him."

"HER RECORDS ARE SEALED, man." Rick winced at the murderous expression that crept across Randy's face.

"And that means, what?" Randy glanced at Emma, who was standing beside her husband. "That whatever's going on is at a level even you can't access?"

"It most likely means that me snooping into Robyn Nobles's life is putting people at risk," Rick explained. "This woman and her baby, if no one else. Someone's got to have a pretty good reason for there being no record of her anywhere, except a note not to pursue information."

It wasn't the answer Randy had been hoping for. A jealous ex. An abusive husband. Someone Sam had been running from last night, and months ago, that could be stopped from causing her more trouble. This was about something far worse.

Emma took his hand and squeezed.

"What kind of danger is she in?" Chris asked. He and Charlie had joined them.

"There was a federal marshal on scene," Rick explained. "That much I confirmed from the APD officer's report. Which means Randy's instincts are right—there's reason to question the cause of the accident. Beyond that, all I know for sure is that APD brass has agreed to secure the victim's safety until further notice."

"A federal marshal?" Charlie asked.

"As in federal protection?" Chris added.

Randy hadn't mentioned Dean to anyone but his sister. Now all of his siblings were staring at him, while Rick stared at the floor.

"Did she give you her full name in Savannah?" Rick asked.

"No."

"Give you any idea where she was from? If she was married? Why she would be passing through

Atlanta with South Georgia plates that trace back to a dead end?"

"I don't know!" Randy shook off Emma's hold. "We just… It never got that far. All I remember is that there was a northern accent. Not much of one, but it stuck out in a place like Savannah."

And it had been sexy as hell.

"What kind of northern accent?" Rick asked. "Like New York?"

"Maybe." Randy waited for his brother-in-law to say something else, but Rick hesitated. "Just say it. What do you think all this means?"

"With federal marshals involved? I'd guess she's hiding from something or someone that's coming at her from wherever she's originally from. And the feds are interested enough in whatever she knows to keep her hidden."

"You're saying this woman's been on the run since March?" Chris sputtered.

"Maybe longer." Rick rolled his shoulders beneath his Atlanta Braves T-shirt. "Not that we're ever going to know."

"Why?" Charlie asked.

"Depending on what she's offering in return for protection," Rick said. "She might be—"

"Running for the rest of her life," Randy finished.

The possibility of federal relocation made Sam's disappearance from his arms that morning go down a little easier. But it also made everything he didn't know about her situation harder to stomach. Not to mention that he might be responsible for the innocent, newborn life she'd have with her from now on.

"Excuse me, folks." Seth Washington stepped into the lounge.

Atlanta Memorial's chief of staff was another family friend—by way of having bonded with Emma's husband when they'd both gotten sucked into helping an FBI deep cover agent who'd landed in Emergency. Rick crossed the room to shake the man's hand.

"I'm sorry to have to be the one to tell you this." Seth shifted his attention to Randy. "But I knew you were waiting for news about the patient you rode in with, and I didn't want Kate to have to deliver it. We had her stabilized, but there were complications with the delivery, and—"

"The baby?" The strain in Randy's voice made it unrecognizable to his own ears.

"A girl. She's a week or two premature, and there were some breathing issues at first. But she's responding well now and shouldn't even need to stay the night in neonatal ICU. I imagine she'll be moved to the general nursery in a matter of hours. Unfortunately, the mother's hemorrhaging was beyond our ability to—"

"Sam…" Randy's relief at the news about the baby choked in his throat. "She's…"

"I'm sorry, Randy," Seth said while Emma, Chris and Charlie stepped closer. "I'm afraid she's gone."

RANDY STOOD at the nursery window of Atlanta General's pediatric wing, staring blindly at the tiny lives being nurtured inside. He didn't even know if Sam's baby was in there. And he had absolutely no right to ask. But the invisible pull that had lured him here had been stronger than logic.

What the hell was he doing?

"I haven't seen you this shut down," Emma said beside him, "since…"

"Since we lost Mom," he finished for her. The last thing he'd felt this strongly had been grief over their mother's death, which had come less than a year after she'd killed their father—to keep the bastard from ever threatening her kids again. "Mom gave up her freedom and then her life to protect us."

"It sounds like your Sam was fighting just as hard to protect her baby."

His Sam.

"You can't save everyone," Emma insisted gently.

No one had tried to persuade him to leave the hospital. His brothers had let him be, walking away with parting slaps of support on Randy's shoulder. Emma had wanted to talk with Seth a little more. And Randy had somehow ended up at the nursery.

Of course Emma had found him there. When she'd been barely more than a teenager herself, she'd fought to get Randy and his brothers back from the different foster homes they'd been scattered to. No way was his big sister leaving Randy alone to face this, even if no one could tell them exactly what *this* was.

"She wasn't just another victim," he said, finally verbalizing the ache that had been gnawing at him since Seth's news. "She…"

"Was someone you knew for less than a day! Stop torturing yourself over something that isn't your responsibility."

If only it were that simple.

He wished to God it *was* that simple.

"She begged me to protect her daughter." Kate had relayed the message that Sam had still been terrified in the delivery room. Asking for Randy by name and insisting he had to save their baby from some unseen evil that was closing in. "She said they were in danger."

"She was in shock. Look around you." Emma gestured at the early-morning calm of the hallway. "Does it look like anyone thinks a baby's in danger? Where is that marshal you said was on scene? Why hasn't Seth heard anything about any of this? He runs this place. If there was really a problem—"

"Sam said her little girl is mine." It was the only reality that mattered right now. "I don't know which I want to be less true—that a baby might be alone and in danger because I couldn't save her mother, or that I might be the father of an infant who has no one else in the world to look after her but me."

"You don't know that her baby is alone now."

"No. But I know that Sam didn't want someone named Luca to get anywhere near the child."

"Then what are you doing just standing here, staring off into space?" Emma's smack on his shoulder wasn't nearly as encouraging as their brothers' had been. "You've harassed Kate and me to get people to pull strings for you and find out who this woman is. That didn't pan out, but you're clearly not ready to move on. If you think you should have a say in what happens to her baby, if you feel obligated to step in, then do what you have to do to make that happen."

Randy closed his eyes, hating the growing impulse to walk away before he grew even more attached.

"And if a paternity test turns out to be positive?" he asked.

Protect her, Randy.

Don't let him destroy our child, too…

"Then you and I will be taking your beautiful daughter home as soon as her doctors will let us." Emma's features turned somber, as if she could sense how much he was mourning Sam, on top of his confusion about his responsibility to her child.

Emma more than anyone else understood Randy's inability to process that kind of connection to another person. She'd almost lost Rick over her own battle with the same fear. Then her expression grew determined.

"Man up, Montgomery," she said. "It's time to crack that hero's heart of yours open and join the rest of us in the emotional uncertainty we like to call reality."

"LUCA'S GOING TO FIND ME!" Sam struggled to sit up in her hospital bed, shrugging off the confusion that had clouded her mind since she woke.

Every move she made hurt. The pain meds weren't making a dent. Not that it mattered. If she didn't fight, she'd die. She hadn't remembered much yet, but one thing was certain—she'd never felt in more danger. And that was saying something.

She looked wildly around the tiny room where they'd hidden her on Atlanta Memorial's psychiatric lockdown ward. Her IV line pulled as she crossed her arms. The needle feeding the vein in the back of her hand pinched.

What was she doing in Atlanta? She was supposed to be hiding in a tiny house on the rural outskirts of Macon. She'd been in a car accident, that much she knew. But she could only remember the sounds of crashing vehicles, an oppressing sense of panic, then nothing until she'd woken in this bare room.

How long had she been unconscious?

How long had it taken her protection detail to find her?

"What's going on?" she asked for the third time.

"You're clear," Max Dean reassured her, still giving no real answers. "Take it easy so your mind can sort the rest out. The doctors don't want you to push it right away."

Push it?

There was something she should be remembering. Something terrible. Life or death.

"I'm clear? Of Luca?" Luca she could remember. No one was ever clear of him. Sam laughed, and her head nearly exploded. "You've got to be kidding."

The doctor who'd been there when Sam regained consciousness a few minutes ago had said she'd be sore for several days, but none of her injuries were life-threatening. It was a miracle, he'd added, after her blood pressure had bottomed out. They almost hadn't gotten her back. But there was no reason to worry about the short-term memory loss. If she took it easy, the concussion would ease and she'd recover everything before long.

Sam rubbed her temple, careful to avoid the gash that had been stitched back together. The few sketchy details her marshal had given her weren't enough. Not nearly enough.

"Your death ends this," Max explained. "Whoever looks will find evidence that your injuries were fatal. It's a fact. All you have to do now is relax until you're ready to remember the rest."

"The rest?"

Max was always there to clean up whatever mess she made of her protection. He even looked a little relieved to see her alive—and maybe not just because losing her would have damaged his spotless record at the U.S. Marshals Service. But he was also watching her as if he expected her to fall apart at any second.

If she was "clear" and his team had taken care of everything, why was *he* so worried still?

"It's only been an hour since they treated you," he hedged. "Give it time."

"But I'm… You're telling everyone I'm dead. How…"

"The O.R. staff was interviewed. The hospital powers that be are on board. Robyn Nobles is dead. Catastrophic injuries incurred during a fatal hit-and-run. Any record to the contrary, here or with the fire and rescue team, will be dealt with. My team's already on it. Stop worrying. Stop running. Let me and my team do our jobs, Sam."

Running...

Sam had been driving. Someone had been chasing her. And...she'd been in pain, even before she crashed into the guardrail, then into another car. And in the O.R.... She'd been screaming in pain that hadn't been from her injuries. There'd been...

A delivery nurse?

Sam's hands flew to her now-soft belly.

"My baby!" A nurse had told Sam everything would be okay. And Sam had said... What? "I had my baby? But... Where is she? Why can't I remember?"

"You will," Max assured her. "All that's important now is that you're okay, and so is the baby. I asked the doctor not to tell you anything—"

"You what!"

"Worrying you until you were ready wasn't going to accomplish anything. You need to rest and recover, Sam, so we can get you moving. My people are taking care of your daughter's cover story. The records will show that she died, too. There will be another report that an unnamed child was left outside the E.R. tonight. She'll be admitted to the pediatric unit, once she's released from ICU."

"ICU!" Sam's thoughts wouldn't stay focused. They kept tangling all over themselves and Max's half truths and the huge hole still in her memory.

How could she have forgotten she'd delivered her daughter? She couldn't remember having her. Holding her. Making sure she was okay.

"You said she's fine," Sam said. "Then why is she in ICU? What's wrong?"

"She's a little premature, and they're taking precautions because of the accident, nothing more. For all I know, they've already moved her. One of my deputies is keeping an eye on the situation, but there's no reason to think anyone will be looking for your child. There's nothing to trace her to you. She'll be safe in foster care until—"

"Until someone who saw me deliver her says the wrong thing to the wrong people and…"

And what?

There was more, but her mind wouldn't grab hold of it.

Sam closed her eyes. Tried to think. Warning bells clamored over everything. What wasn't Max telling her? What hadn't she told him?

"We've explained to the trauma and O.R. staffs that they're under a federal gag order. They'll be arrested if the truth leaks. If Luca is behind your accident, and—"

"It was Luca." The man the federal government was supposed to be protecting her from was closer than ever.

"Then when he investigates what happened tonight, he won't find anything more than your and your baby's death certificates. It's actually a good development. Now he'll call off his dogs."

"You don't know him."

The memories were rushing back, at least the ones from before she'd run. Luca had found her in Macon the same day the travel channel had shown pictures of her. The same day! Only hours after she'd called Gabby.

Which meant he'd already had men close.

Too close.

"He won't stop until he sees my dead body for himself."

"The records show your body was cremated, due to a mix-up in paperwork. We're covering all the bases, Sam. Stop fighting me. This latest stunt of yours means you'll have around-the-clock protection from now on. The grand jury's convening soon. Calm down enough to heal, so you can testify the way the federal prosecutor needs you. Then I'll place you and your daughter in a permanent identity thousands of miles from here. We'll get Gabby to you, too. You'll all be free. But you have to stick to the plan. Stop panicking and screwing up and making it impossible for me to keep you safe."

"Free?" The word felt empty. It felt like fear, because something was still terribly wrong.

"You've been self-destructing from day one." Max sat in the only chair in her stark room. "Let's just call this what it is, Sam. Rock bottom. Having pictures of yourself plastered all over basic cable. Calling Gabby before I could get to you. Running, thinking you could evade your brother's men on your own? You've done just about everything you can to ruin your chances to stay alive long enough to get custody of your sister. But somehow, you're still here. This is your last chance. Don't throw it away like you have all the others."

"You didn't hear Gabby's voice…." But Sam could remember it now. The memory was a horrible, nauseating echo.

Her sister had sounded so much older. Hopeless. Lost, in a way only Sam could understand.

"Actually I did. I receive recordings of all federal taps on your brother's lines." Max's expression bordered on understanding. "But calling like that—causing this mess—only weakens her chances of making it out."

"She's dying there!" Gabriella's faith and trust and hope were dying because Sam had abandoned her. "I was sure I'd never see her again. I had to tell her I love her and I'm fighting for her. That I left because I thought it would protect her."

"Well, to protect her now, you have to stay dead." Max pushed to his feet. "If you want to save her and your baby, you have to lay low, Sam. No more sneaking away from protection like running to Savannah, I don't care how bad the pressure gets or how tired you are of doing nothing for Gabby. No more phone calls. No more leaving me or my men behind. No contact with anyone, including your child. No one can know you're alive except my investigators. You're on lockdown until you testify, or more people are going to die—starting with you."

"But I…" Sam breathed against a rush of tears, hating the pleading in her voice. She clutched her empty belly. "Can't I just hold her? Just once?"

She could finally remember saying the same thing

to the delivery nurse. She could remember the loneliness consuming her. Sam's arms felt even emptier now.

Max shook his head. He took her hand. A gentle gesture for such a closed-off man.

"What do you think will happen if there's any hint that your child isn't an unnamed orphan?" he asked. "You can't visit her. You can't see her, Sam. You can't check on her, except through my people. No one can know her at all, until Luca is indicted and behind bars."

No one can know her.

The importance of his warning, the panic that followed, released the rest of Sam's memories.

"Oh my God, Randy..."

Randy's face was there now, his voice, filling in the gaps she couldn't remember about the accident. Moments that still felt like hazy dreams, except they were real.

He'd really been there. She'd really told him, and—

"The nurse," she whispered. "I told the delivery nurse, too, because she seemed to know him... Oh my God, Max. What have I done?"

"Randy who?" Max was already dialing on his cell. The familiar calm of his voice was gone. An emotionless mask consumed his expression. "Do you mean that firefighter? Lieutenant Randall Montgomery? He wouldn't talk to me. What did you tell him and your nurse, Sam? Think!"

"When I was still in the car... He was there, and I thought I was dying. And in the O.R.... I asked her to get a message to him, in case you didn't protect the baby…. I thought I was dreaming, or that I was going to die and it was the only way, or… I don't know what I thought! Except that I had to protect our daughter. I had to—"

"*Our* daughter?" Max's eyes closed, then reopened. "The rescue team lead who insisted on riding in the ambulance with you. *He's* your hookup in Savannah? Your baby's father?"

What do you think will happen if there's any hint that your child isn't an unnamed orphan…

"I told him, Max." No matter how hard she tried to protect everyone, to make up for the mistakes she'd made, no matter how hard she fought, she kept making things worse. "I… I told him at the accident."

"Which means while my men are trying to cover your tracks," Max said, "your firefighter will be looking to take *his* daughter home with him. And there won't be anything I can do to stop him without calling even more attention to the situation."

CHAPTER SIX

RANDY REACHED into the backseat of Emma's car and lifted the baby seat from its detachable base. The sleeping little girl strapped inside gave a threatening wiggle. When she didn't wake, Randy sent a thankful look skyward.

"Do they always scream like that?" he asked the only woman in his life who'd cared for an infant.

"Car rides usually settle babies down." Emma had the nerve to chuckle. "Jessie was a motion junkie. Some nights when she wouldn't settle in, I'd put her in the car and drive until she conked out. Your little one seems to be more of the cries-herself-out type. Lucky for you—" Emma glanced back before unlocking the door of his ground floor condo "—I think she's exhausted herself."

"So she'll sleep through the night now?"

Randy, who dodged fires and charged into catastrophe for a living, felt himself shaking at the thought of dealing with a screaming, inconsolable baby again before morning. Facing his memories of Sam wouldn't be any easier.

He hadn't been able to save her, but thanks to an

expedited paternity test he had a chance at making things right with their daughter. Except, what did he know about cuddling and diaper changing and rocking babies to sleep? His custody was only temporary for now, but the legality of things didn't matter. He had a responsibility to Sam's child. *His* child. He was going to fulfill it. Just as soon as he figured out what the hell he was doing.

Emma laughed at his lame question and whatever expression had crossed his face.

"I don't know how to break it to you," she said. "But neither of you will be sleeping much for a while. Most newborns eat every two hours or so. Especially ones who need to put on a few pounds before their ten-day checkup."

"What's a ten-day checkup?"

Randy had signed every piece of paper the hospital gave him. He'd listened carefully to the nurse's post-natal list of dos and don'ts. But the nonstop screaming until they were halfway home had obliterated everything he'd learned. It felt like his brain was bleeding out of his ears.

"Don't worry." Emma led the way inside, passing the foyer's lights without flipping them on. "When she wakes, give her one of the single-serving bottles the hospital sent home. I'll go over the rest with you tomorrow."

"Tomorrow!"

Emma was leaving?

Of course she was. She had a teenager and a husband to get back to.

"I guess…" He guessed, what? That he had no right to whine about his responsibilities to a woman who'd never balked at her own? "I'm sure I'll be fine on my own until tomorrow?"

Stumbling forward with the baby carrier, he fumbled for the light switch. The glare blinded him. It took several seconds to focus on the crowd overflowing his living room—fronted by a beaming Emma, who was now cuddled into her brawny husband's arms.

"Surprise!" everyone faux-screamed in whispered voices.

"What the fu—"

"Language, little brother," Emma chastised. "Did you really think we'd let this moment pass without some acknowledgment? It's been a rough twenty-four hours, I know, but you're a father. Oh, my gosh, Randy." Her eyes filled. She rubbed a finger under her nose as she sniffed. "My baby brother's a father."

Her mini-breakdown was evidently the cue everyone had been waiting for. Within seconds, Randy was surrounded by quiet congratulations and hugs of support and encouragement, all delivered without waking the tiny noise box he still carried. It was disconcerting, unsettling, surreal—having his family and several of the guys from the firehouse looking at him as though he might freak out if they didn't keep their positive faces on.

Even more disconcerting was how his heart stalled when Emma took the carrier from him so she could change the baby's diaper. Just that brief loss of contact with his daughter, and Randy had to stop himself from following his sister.

His panic made no sense. Except there was still so much up in the air. Way too much that didn't make sense.

"You doing okay, man?" A hand closed on his shoulder.

Randy jumped before he realized it was Charlie.

"Sure." His gaze followed Emma's escape into the quiet of his bedroom. "It's going to take some getting used to, but it's all good, right?"

That had been their lifelong mantra, him and his brothers. But since the accident, Randy startled at the slightest sound. He couldn't get over the sense that something was still terribly wrong, or the shock of knowing he'd never see Sam again.

All was definitely *not* good.

"Hang in there." Charlie's hand squeezed. "We're all here for you, man. Every step of the way."

"Yeah."

His brothers and sister would have his back. And since they were kids, that had always been enough. But now… It was like there was an emptiness inside Randy he didn't have a clue how to fill. Not when he could still see the fear that had been in Sam's eyes when she'd begged him to protect their daughter from danger that had never materialized.

Except that Sam was dead, and Randy couldn't stand to have their child out of his sight for even a few minutes.

"Say, Charlie," he said. "Do me a favor?"

"Anything."

"If something happens… Do whatever you have to to protect the baby."

"What's going to happen?" Charlie's voice lowered. He stepped closer. "Whatever this Sam was mixed up in, there's no way the authorities would have let you take the baby home if there was still a risk."

"Yeah, I know." Except Randy didn't know. Not everything. And it was bugging the hell out of him. "I guess I just need a good night's sleep. Then—"

The doorbell interrupted.

More people?

"So much for being a lonely bachelor, huh?" Charlie slapped Randy's shoulder with a bit more enthusiasm than was necessary, then headed toward a group of their friends by the fireplace.

If Randy's family didn't stop trying to *comfort* him, he was going to be black and blue.

"Bet you were hoping for a quiet night at home?" Chris called as Randy headed for the foyer.

Randy laughed at his brother's familiar ribbing. It felt good. Solid. Maybe things were going to be fine after all.

The impromptu party ramped up behind him as he opened the door.

The bastard on his doorstep was wearing the same suit and tie as when Randy had last seen him on a rainy interstate.

"Dean," Randy said to the federal marshal.

He didn't have to turn around to know Chris and Charlie had joined them. The marshal flashed his badge for Randy's brothers' benefit.

"What's this about?" Charlie wanted to know.

"I'm afraid I'm not at liberty to say." Dean looked around the three of them to the crowd of spectators quieting down to watch. "I'm going to have to insist that Lieutenant Montgomery and his daughter come with me immediately."

"You can insist all you want," Charlie said while Randy measured the steel in the federal marshal's even gaze. "Doesn't mean my brother or his child are moving an inch from this apartment."

The baby cried from the direction of the bedroom. Randy turned to see his sister walk back into the den with a blanket-swaddled bundle on her shoulder. He caught how the federal marshal's frown deepened as he stared at the child.

"What's wrong?" Randy asked.

"That baby was never supposed to leave the hospital." Nothing moved in the man's expression. "But we couldn't stop you, once you set the paternity issue in motion. Not until you and the child were settled in a less public arena. Now, the longer it's here, the more danger you're putting everyone in."

It?

"Well, there's no way you're removing *her* from my care." A surge of protectiveness shot through Randy. Every muscle in his body was vibrating.

"Obviously." Dean didn't blink. "Shall we go?"

The skin on the back of Randy's neck tingled.

The man was serious about the danger he thought Randy and his daughter were still in.

Promise me... Protect her, Randy. Don't let him destroy our child, too....

"What's wrong?" Randy asked again.

"Robyn Nobles's baby isn't safe here, which means neither are any of you."

"You mean Sam's baby?"

Dean eyed Randy and his brawny brothers without answering.

"She's perfectly healthy," Emma insisted. She joined the group at the door and handed Randy his daughter when he couldn't stop himself from reaching for her. "Otherwise, the hospital wouldn't have released her so soon."

"The baby was released quickly, because my office requested it," Max countered. "And because we assured the hospital staff that the child would have round-the-clock care once we placed her in protective custody."

"Why wouldn't my brother's baby be safe at home with her family?" Emma asked.

"Because you aren't her only family," the federal marshal explained, while once again not explaining anything. "And her existence puts you and your relatives at severe risk, Mrs. Downing. My assistant will explain everything—" a woman in a severely stylish pantsuit, wearing the same emotionally shutdown expression as Dean, stepped to his side "—once Lieutenant Montgomery and the child are in my care. I'm afraid this is not a request. Your actions have jeopardized a federal case, which means I don't need your cooperation to take you into custody."

"Custody?" Rick Downing joined his wife. "On what grounds?"

"Perhaps protection is a better term," Dean's assistant offered.

"Whatever you call it—" Randy reminded himself that his daughter was what was important now, not his growing impatience with how completely his well-ordered life had gone to shit "—I'm not agreeing to a damn thing until you tell us what you think you're *protecting* us from."

"Either come voluntarily—" irritation chipped away at Dean's control "—or I arrest your ass and drag you and your daughter away while your family and friends watch. Gather whatever you need to care for the child for the next hour or so. We'll pick up the rest on the road. You have five minutes."

"I'm not going anywhere with you!" Randy's raised voice unsettled the sleeping baby.

She began to whimper, then cry. He patted clumsily at her back, tempted to scream along with her.

"Yes, you are, Lieutenant." A hint of apology warmed Dean's eyes as he watched Randy's feeble attempt at fatherhood. "If you care about your family at all, you'll walk away right now, before your resistance gets them all killed."

"I HAVE TO GET Gabby!" Sam wouldn't leave without Gabriella. "Not now. Not after—"

"You can't go back. You're a threat to everyone

you care about. No contact is the only choice, until Luca's neutralized."

"But she's my sister! She's all I have left."

"If you love her, you'll walk away."

"No!"

"Sam, calm down. You came to us. Wake up and see the danger you're in. Do the only thing that keeps you and your sister safe. Wake up, Sam... Sam..."

"Sam... Wake up. Sam!"

She jerked from the dream. She squinted against the glare from the bedside table's lamp. Max was standing over her.

Sitting up was a mistake. Pain ripped down her arm from her injured shoulder. Her head was on fire where she'd been stitched up. Where was she? Her hand slipped to her belly. No baby. No! Where was her daughter? What had happened? What—

Reality flashed back, faster this time. But the rush wasn't any less painful. Her baby and Randy were gone. All Max had said when he'd left her room on the psych ward was that he'd handle her latest screw-up—somehow. The next morning, his deputies had gotten Sam into a car once her doctor released her, though she was still hooked up to an IV. They'd driven her God knew where. Not that she cared about anything but what she was leaving behind.

She could do this, she reminded herself. Starting over—again. She'd keep fighting until Luca was out of her life for good. As long as she knew the people she cared about were safe, she could do this. And she'd do it right this time.

"How long has she been out?" Max asked someone.

"She fell asleep as soon as we got here," a woman responded—the female marshal whose job seemed to be to watch Sam breathe.

Sam lost her battle to keep her eyes open and slumped back to the pillows.

"Do you really think it's wise to have them both in one place?" the woman asked.

"You got any better ideas?" Max challenged. "Whatever it takes to keep this situation from blowing apart further, that's what we're doing today."

Sam's head was going to explode if they didn't stop arguing.

"Please," she said, "take your *Sam's a total screw-up* conversation into the other room, before—"

A baby's cry pierced through her pounding head. Through her heart. She pushed herself to sit at the edge of the bed.

The tacky hotel room spun around her until she blinked it into focus. And there he was: a tall, bewildered-looking man standing just inside the bedroom's door, holding a squirming baby girl as if he didn't quite know what to do with her.

"Randy?"

He said something. Something Sam couldn't hear over the disgruntled sounds being made by the beautiful creature in his arms. Randy stared back at her, his expression hardening. He took a step closer, a hand reaching out as if he wasn't completely sure she was real. But Sam cringed away.

It must still be a dream—Randy and their daughter standing in front of her.

No, it was a nightmare!

"Get her away from me," Sam begged as the shadows closed in. She clenched her fists until her nails dug into her skin. The pain kept her from grabbing her daughter close and never letting her go.

Then there was only darkness. The feeling of a strong, familiar grip catching her. The emptiness of knowing that her baby was safer anywhere but with her.

CHAPTER SEVEN

"…WRONG WITH HER?" the voice was saying. "Sam? Wake up, baby."

Baby.

Randy…

Her mind slipped away from a reality she couldn't face. The dream she'd been having was better. A dream of Randy calling her baby, their one night together.

"Tell me your name, baby." Magical hands were molding her body, sending sensation sizzling up her spine and outward to every nerve ending, until there was more pleasure than should be possible…

"I don't even know your name." His teeth nipped the sensitive curve of her neck.

"Isn't it wonderful?" She curled into his body, wrapping herself up in the anonymity they'd agreed to.

"It's… You're amazing." He cupped her waist, his words slurring when she knew for a fact that he was stone-cold sober.

She'd watched him party with his buddies. St. Patrick's Day in Savannah was a crazy, all-day celebration. A southern-fried Mecca calling pilgrims from hundreds of miles away. All were welcome—

anyone, that is, who wanted to cut loose and revel and get stupid drunk until they stumbled back to their hotels. But Randy, the only name she'd let him give her, had clearly been the designated Boy Scout of his group, in charge of keeping the other guys out of jail while they got their wild on.

He'd had only one beer that she'd seen, while he'd spent most of the day staring at her from the doorway of a pub across the street. She'd watched him back from her table beside a River Street bistro. A bottle of wine of her own later, one of Randy's disarming smiles, and she'd agreed to meet him in the lobby of his hotel. Not that wine was all that had driven her to this recklessness.

Stretched above her on his bed, he was every predatory and possessive and protective dream she'd ever had. But he was also easing away.

"Where are you going?" She clung to him.

When she sat up, the sexually rumpled woman reflecting back at her from the mirrored bureau was a stranger. He tugged the hand she reached toward him to his lips and gave it a kiss.

"An A-bomb couldn't move me from this bed." His chuckle was a sinful thing. And in the charming smile that followed, Sam caught a glimpse of the devilish boy he must have once been. "But you have to tell me your name. I want to do things to you I have no business wanting with someone I have to call baby."

"I don't mind being your baby tonight." She traced a nail across his bottom lip, then slipped her

fingers under the collar of his Grateful Dead T-shirt. Then across crisp hair that was a shade darker than the thick waves of golden brown covering his head. "That's what we said, right? Just tonight?"

"Just tonight." His touch tickled and tantalized beneath the neckline of her sundress. He'd done this before. He was a master at it. "So, you're not a woman looking for relationship drama?"

"God, no!" No more drama.

"Me neither." He was just a simple country guy in town for a good time, he'd assured her. "No interest in more than one night?"

Her head shook once.

Her bangs fluttered into her eyes.

"Now is all I have," she whispered.

He seemed fascinated with the effect her next breath had on the cleavage spilling out of her loosened dress. "So tomorrow it's back to the real world you left behind when you decided to make my weekend coming down here?"

"Something like that."

"Wherever you're going, it's gotta be far from here. A woman like you doesn't belong in a small town like this." Coming from another man, it might have been an insult. But somehow this stranger's wicked glance down her body and back up again made Sam feel cherished for who she was—even though he knew absolutely nothing about her. "A woman like you belongs in a pampered penthouse on top of some Manhattan skyscraper."

He'd asked more than once where she was from.

How did she tell him she didn't belong anywhere anymore, and most definitely not New York?

He stroked her breast. His brown eyes sparked to flame as his thumb found her nipple.

"Okay, we'll forget about where home is. Just give me a name." He edged down the flimsy strap of her sundress. Lowered his head. "Otherwise, I'm afraid I might have to stop and—"

"S...Sam..." The name slipped past her control, because he couldn't stop. She couldn't bear it.

It was just a first name. She'd never see him again after tonight. There were no ties between them. She and Gabby would still be safe.

"My name is Sam."

"Now, was that so hard?" His hands slid down her back, arching her spine. "Let's get more comfortable, Sam, my girl."

From one blink to the next, her dress was down to her waist. His mouth feasted on the breasts she hadn't bothered covering with a bra in the Low Country heat. Her own hands rode up his sides and around the shocking ridges of hard muscle beneath his shirt, until she could tug him closer. His body covered the skin his mouth had left glistening. She captured his lips with her own and allowed her mind to wander while her legs skimmed around his hips to cradle where he was hardest against where she needed him most...

"Sam... Baby..."

"...Sam? Baby, wake up..."

His touch was warm on her cheek. His voice felt

closer than her dreams. So were the sweet newborn baby sounds layering over the memory.

Randy's deep voice mixing with her baby's sweet cries… Sam curled on her side, wanting to hold the moment close. A shock of pain streaked through her body, the reality of it unraveling the last of the dream.

"Don't go," she cried, desperate to hold on to the memories.

She smoothed her hand protectively down her flat belly. She jerked awake, her entire body shaking.

"My baby. Where's my baby?"

"Shh." His voice sounded so far away now.

His voice.

Randy's voice.

He was really there, sitting beside her and holding a squirming blanket that was emitting endearing whimpers that made Sam's blood freeze in her veins.

"Get out of here," she gasped, remembering everything. Again.

She was getting sick and tired of reality taking its sweet time coming back to her, every time her body chose to let her down.

Enough with the useless dreams.

Think, Sam!

She was safe, in a hotel. On the outskirts of Atlanta. As far as Max's team could transport her until they were sure her condition had stabilized. But it wasn't far enough, evidently. Luca had a very good chance of discovering that she and her daughter had survived. Sam would be disappearing again, so no one else got hurt because of her. Except her protection had decided to bring the people most likely to pay for her dangerous choices closer.

"And you call me reckless!" Sam glared at Max, who was frowning beside Randy. "Why would you bring them here?"

Randy looked so strong and solid and real, sitting beside her on the bed. Sam closed her eyes against the crisp hint of his aftershave that was mixing with their baby's sweet, newborn smell.

The doctors had administered a drug to counteract the hormones that would have allowed her to nurse. She'd accepted the reality that she couldn't see her daughter's father again. That it was best if she left her child to be cared for by strangers.

Except there they were, Randy and their daughter, close enough for Sam to touch.

"Are…are you okay?" Randy's voice held the same forced calmness as it had when he'd reached inside her wrecked car and rescued her.

"No."

Sam couldn't bear it. She couldn't stop herself. She grabbed their baby from him and clutched the little girl to her chest.

"Oh, God. I thought I'd never see her," she said into the soft crown of dark brown curls atop her daughter's head. They were her father's curls. "A part of me was so sure I'd never get to hold her."

Sam and Randy's gazes locked. He wiped away the tears clinging to the corners of her eyes. His hand was shaking. The growing confusion—outrage?—on his face threatened an explosion any second.

"They told me you were dead." Accusation crowded out the softness in his voice.

"She is." Max nodded for the woman who'd been watching Sam to head into the adjoining room. "And her child was never born. At least, that was our plan until you claimed paternity of Baby Doe. We had to let it happen so we didn't get more hospital staff involved. Letting your family take the heat for your decision was easier to contain, once you took the baby home. You were never out of the sight of my team. None of you will be from now on, until this is settled."

RANDY STOOD. It was no doubt wrong to take pleasure in looming over Sam's federal marshal by a good three inches.

Screw wrong.

He didn't have the first clue what was going on or how he was supposed to handle it. He hadn't had his emotional footing for over twenty-four hours, and feeling powerless was getting old.

"And just what the hell was your plan for *my* child," he demanded, intentionally excluding Sam for the moment and knowing it would hurt her. That was just too damn bad. He kept his gaze on Dean. "What would you have done if I hadn't listened to my family and had the good sense to confirm my child's paternity before you could get your lying hands on her?"

"We certainly would have kept you and your family from putting yourselves and your baby at risk. Unfortunately, that's no longer an option." The marshal looked down at Sam.

Randy couldn't keep his own gaze from following. She was a bruised and battered mess, with one arm in a sling and the other hooked to an IV. And she only had eyes for the baby she was holding, which for some reason made him even more furious. Didn't she care that he felt like an idiot for being played like this? Why wasn't she terrified of the anger building inside him, because of how the sudden appearance of her and her secrets had ripped into his life?

"I'll be in the next room." Dean turned to go. "My team will be working out contingency strategies. Get this guy on board, Sam. Stick to the basics, but get it done."

"But—" Sam looked up.

"Do it!" The marshal headed into the adjoining room.

"This guy?" A part of Randy wanted to settle back onto the bed and hold Sam, until all he could feel was the crazy things that happened to him every time she was close.

Instead, he forced himself to remember his shock and panic when he'd been told she was dead. The agony of deciding to do the right thing by their child. The fear on his brothers' and sister's faces when a federal marshal had dragged Randy and the baby away.

"You dump all this, whatever *this* is, in my lap, complete with a baby—*my* baby—who I took in, no matter how much being a father was going to screw with my life. And now I'm just 'this guy'?"

Sam flinched, but she didn't look away from their

daughter. A part of him was afraid for her still, even though they were surrounded by feds. She looked like what she was—a woman who'd been in a multicar pileup, then she'd had to deliver a baby for her troubles. And now there he was, demanding the answers he was due, while Dean left her to clean up the mess his people had helped make. A softer man would have apologized and calmed down.

But Randy knew better. No matter how small and defenseless Sam looked, there was strength there that he wouldn't underestimate again. A fierceness that he'd been instantly drawn to, when what he should have done was walk away. This woman was a fighter. A scrappy survivor in a passel of trouble who'd do whatever she had to, to cover her ass.

"Are you okay enough to hold her?" he asked reluctantly.

"I...I think so." She sounded anything but okay. She was terrified.

What scared her most? Him? Them? Or whatever evil had forced her into a situation where the suits in the next room had the right to run her life? Meanwhile the protection Dean and his deputies were supposed to be giving her seemed to be failing at every possible turn.

Randy clenched his fists. It was ridiculous, the feeling he couldn't shake that they belonged together. That he belonged in the middle of this mess with Sam. Beside her.

"She's so tiny," Sam said with a sense of awe.

"Didn't you get to hold her when..." When what? "I mean, before?"

Sam shook her head.

"Everything happened so fast." Her tone was almost as dead as Dean's had been. "One minute I was delivering her. The next time I woke up, she was gone. Then Max was gone, too…dealing with you and your family…" She couldn't seem to catch her breath. "Our baby would be safe right now, if neither of us were in her life. That sounds horrible…but it's true. But I was so scared at the accident. I let myself forget… I'm so sorry, Randy, for everything. I never should have gotten you and your family messed up in this. Max never should have brought you here. I…"

She was sorry. About them. About the baby. Their daughter, who would be better off in Sam's mind, if she was with neither of her parents. He'd been longing to comfort her. Now he wanted to shake her.

"Exactly where is *here?*" he demanded. He'd been too preoccupied with the baby to pay close attention on the drive over. "Because like it or not, Marshal Dean thought this was a good idea. And I'm getting damn tired of not having a clue about what's happening to my life!"

For a second, he thought she was trembling and he almost felt guilty about it. Then he thought she was giggling. Tiny, almost silent bursts of laughter seemed to be leaking out of her as she held their daughter tighter.

Furious, he tipped her head up to find silent tears streaming down her face.

"Damn it," he whispered. The weight of his unwanted feelings for this woman and the child they'd made together settled deeper.

"What's happening to *your* life?" Her next laugh was more of a sob. "You're not that blind. None of this is about your life."

She scrubbed the back of one hand across her eyes. She gave the baby a gentle kiss, then handed her back to Randy. A flash of pain crossed her face as she move her injured arm, but she didn't make a sound.

"This is about me and my own personal security team," she said. "And me running from a world that's so messed up, it makes me invaluable to the people who pay Max's salary." She looked at Randy holding their child, and tears filled her eyes once again. "It's about me wanting something good and clean and miles away from everything I know, and there you were. And here you are. Again."

Randy didn't want to hear this. He didn't want to be part of her emotional breakdown, meanwhile she'd prefer that he didn't exist.

"Just spit it out," he said, feeling stronger somehow now that he had his daughter back in his arms. "Dean obviously wants me in the know, or he wouldn't have brought me here. And whatever I thought in Savannah, it's clear I know nothing about who you really are. Except that you have a past you're ashamed of. Believe it or not, that might be the one thing we have in common. So enough with the smoke and mirrors. Just how bad is it?"

Sam scooted back against her pillows. Her IV line pulled tight. She flexed and relaxed her fingers, looking too exhausted to be sitting at all. He stayed away, worried for her and resenting it while the silence between them grew. His sister and brothers were what he should be worried about. His daughter, who Sam was clearly in no position to make her priority.

"How bad is it?" she finally said. "You had a life in Atlanta. A career. Friends. Family. Now—"

"Had?"

Sam flinched.

"Max the Wonder Marshal scared my family to death to get me here," Randy said. "He was pretty damn convincing, saying that everyone I cared about would be in danger if the baby and I stayed with them. Are you going to tell me the rest, or do I get to beat it out of Dean? Come to think of it, that might be my favorite alternative."

Sam sat taller and squared her shoulders, then winced in pain.

"My family kills for a living," she said as calmly as if she was discussing the cold front that had moved in. "That's why yours is in danger now. That's why there is no end to this for any of you, not anytime soon."

"Your family…" Randy looked down at his daughter and for the first time believed that her life really might be in danger. "Is…"

"One of the largest organized crime families still in New York. And I'm the only person who can stop them. Which makes anyone close to me, anyone I care about, a target until the bastard who killed my fiancé goes to prison for the rest of his life. And I'm not stopping until he does."

RANDY STARED at Sam. He'd stepped back, holding their baby farther away. Watching him accept that she was a threat should have been a simple matter of doing what had to be done. Fighting for the right ending to all this—the one Dean said would keep them safe.

But how did she let go of the only dream she still had?

Randy crossed the room and leaned against the desk Max and his deputies had covered with the equipment that was supposed to be jamming cell frequencies or checking for surveillance devices or God knew what else.

"What is your family mixed up in, exactly?" he asked.

"Does it matter?" She refused to let apology or any other emotion creep into her voice. "Not that I know, really. Except that everyone I've known since birth is up to their eyeballs in it. Everyone but my baby sister. We're both a part of it, though. Everything that's happened, Gabby and I have always been a part of it."

"Gabby?"

"Gabriella. She's why I agreed to do this. They promised to get her out."

"What exactly did you agree to do? What happened to warrant all this security? How long have you been living like this?"

"Two years." Sam closed her eyes, not wanting to answer the rest of his questions. But she owed Randy the truth, as much as Max would let her tell. And Randy deserved his say, if that's what it took to get him to take the baby away. "Two years ago, I was sleeping next to my fiancé when Luca shot him."

Randy cuddled their daughter against his chest.

"You've been doing this for two years?" he asked.

"I agreed to do it for as long as it takes. The federal prosecutor said a grand jury appearance might be all they'd need from me, but I'm not buying it. I'll have to face Luca in open court, then I'll disappear for good. I'll have Gabby with me then, and I'll be free of all this. At least that was the plan."

"Luca who?"

Sam looked away and sighed. She shook her head. "The more you know, the greater the risk you'll get even more mixed up in this. You knowing could damage the case. You could be called in to testify."

She pushed herself to her feet. Her legs wobbled. Putting one foot in front of the other wasn't an option yet, but neither was staying in the same room as Randy. Not now that he was staring at her as if she was the enemy.

"This was my choice, Lieutenant. I approached the federal prosecutor and demanded protection for me and my sister. Since then, I've made one mistake after another. Now I've sucked you and our child into my mess. I don't blame you for anything you're thinking about me. So please, just—"

"Mistake? Like sleeping with me?"

"No." Sam sank back to the bed. "That was… Being with you was the only peaceful night I've spent in a long time."

"And our child?" He stepped closer, towering over her. "Is our child another part of this that you regret?"

Sam clutched her hand against her belly.

"I would do anything for my daughter."

"Anything but admitting she exists to her father, until you had no choice. Anything but allowing me a choice in what to do about all this, until it was too late and you'd brought the mob down on my family. *My* family, Sam. Nothing is more important to me, and that now includes my daughter. Don't for a second think I'm letting you take her away from me again!"

It was everything Sam had expected, every horrible word of it. Randy, on the other hand, looked shocked, as if he couldn't quite believe the commitment he'd just made.

"N-no," she said. "Of course you'll want the baby with you."

If it wouldn't have involved her falling on her face and needing Randy's help getting up, she'd have run from them both. Her attachment to watching him hold their daughter was growing by the second. He was going to be such an amazing father.

The useless tears were back, the ones that were there each time she woke up confused and had to remember all of this all over again. She wiped at them, but not before Randy saw. His face softened for a second. He took a step closer.

"Don't." Forbidden memories of feeling safe in his arms crept closer. "Don't lose your nerve now, Montgomery, just because some woman you hate leaks out a few tears."

"I…" He stopped. "I don't hate you, Sam."

But he did. He was a good man, but even good men had their limits.

The baby started struggling in his arms. Nuzzling and fussing and making desperate sounds so obvious that even two clueless grownups could figure it out.

"She's hungry," Sam said.

She glared at Randy through the moisture shimmering in her eyes, suddenly despising him for still being there. This would be one more memory that would torture her, but she wouldn't deny herself just one more priceless moment to remember.

She couldn't.

"Give her to me," Sam begged as he struggled to open the diaper bag he'd slung over his shoulder. "Let me feed my baby."

Startled, Randy handed over their child. Then his expression hardened.

"Feed her," he said. "Then I'm taking my daughter as far away from this insanity as I can."

CHAPTER EIGHT

"A BABY!" Luca shouted into his cell phone.

He pounded his fist against the table. The people nearest him in the restaurant jumped but made a point of not looking his way.

Respect.

That's what he received from total strangers. Why couldn't he have even that little bit of control over Sam!

"Everything…um, everything okay?" a waiter asked, water pitcher in hand.

Luca motioned his head for the waiter to beat it.

A baby. Sam had had a baby while she refused his protection. The family's protection. And now she was dead. Or was she? She'd concealed a pregnancy. What else were she and her handlers up to?

His cell lay where he'd slammed it to the table. He picked it up. He was done trusting others to do what needed to be done.

"If there's a baby, there has to be a father. Find him. Find a way to get to him and anyone who's with him. And send someone to Hartsfield Jackson. I'll be landing in Atlanta in eight hours."

"WHAT DO YOU MEAN we can't see Randy, and we can't go back to our lives for the foreseeable future!" Emma demanded.

Charlie pulled his sister to his side, his glance shifting to her husband's. Downing had warned them where letting Randy get more involved in Sam's life could lead. Rick had a protective arm around Emma's daughter, Jessie.

"Ma'am—" began the female marshal who would be in charge of protecting them, including Emma's fifteen-year-old daughter who'd been picked up from school. "I have no information about your brother's circumstances that—"

"—you can give us," Emma parroted back. "But you *can* drag me to this *safe house* and leave me with a scared teenager to comfort, and absolutely no idea what we're all running from. Plus the sketchy assurances of that man who came to my brother's house to tell us that we're all doomed unless we do exactly what you folks say. I suppose I should be thanking you for your candor."

"The less you know, the better for your safety," Glinda assured her. No last name had been given, so Emma had dubbed the deputy *Glinda, the Good Witch.* "Your brother is safe and with our people."

"Like this Sam was safe with you?" Charlie asked. "Wherever she was living before landing in my brother's lap again?"

"This entire situation is the result of a protectee exceeding the boundaries of her relocation plan." Glinda was all-things professional, except for the muscle ticking along her jawline. "And you can see how many lives have been affected by that mistake. Do the smart thing, and don't use her situation as an example of how to proceed."

"Boundaries? Relocation plan? Her situation…" Emma's defiance dissolved into horror. "Is this really the nonsense you're spouting to Randy somewhere right now? Because the backlash you're in store for is going to make this group—" she looked from her husband to Charlie, then Chris and Jessie "—seem like a welcoming committee."

"Your brother will see reason," the good witch started to say, "as soon as—"

"The hell he will." Charlie couldn't imagine anyone less reasonable than the normally controlled man who'd paced a trench in the floor at Atlanta Memorial a little over a day ago.

That man had asked Charlie to have his back and do what was best for his child. Because at the moment, Randy might be too shaken to know what the best thing was on his own.

"If my brother thinks this woman and his baby are in danger…" Emma started to say. She swallowed and grappled for her husband's hand.

"Protecting our niece will trump every precaution you try to drill into Randy," Charlie finished for her. "If you want to control our brother and whatever gut instinct drives his next move, I'd advise getting my sister and me to wherever you have him stashed. Now."

CHAPTER NINE

"HOW IS SHE DOING?" Randy paced across the tiny bedroom, trying not to get hung up on the sight of Sam feeding their daughter one of the bottles of formula.

But he couldn't tear his gaze away.

It was a crazy thing, feeling an instant connection to a woman who'd cringed away when she'd first seen her child. What kind of mother did that? Except she was clinging to their baby now.

This was my choice, Lieutenant...

"How can something so delicate be so strong," Sam said to herself, "after everything she's been through? She's a miracle."

"Yes, she is," Randy bit out, more confused and more fed up by the second. This was the same woman who'd only acknowledged him as her baby's father when she thought she was dying. "And she deserves better than being a pawn in whatever game you're running with your federal agents."

Sam nodded without meeting his gaze. Seeing her accept his assessment of the situation should have reassured him that taking the baby and getting the hell out of Dodge was the right thing to do.

Instead, it made him want to protect Sam from herself.

"You left your kid sister behind." He clung to his anger like a shield against how vulnerable she suddenly seemed. "How much harder could it be to give up your child, right?"

"Sometimes life is about the choices you don't get to make."

Her voice quivered, but he focused on the cold resignation in her words.

"You could have sent one of your G-men to let me know you were pregnant, so I could make my own choices. You could have helped me keep all this away from *my* family, who I'd die for before I abandoned. Why did you even keep the baby if you didn't want me involved and she meant so little to you?"

It was a low blow. But Randy couldn't get over how she'd shrunk away from him and their child. He'd been standing in the doorway, drinking in the sight of her and feeling as if he were finally home for the first time since he was a child, and she'd been gathering her strength to shove him away.

"If you're in so much trouble the feds think it's dangerous for this Luca character to know there's another life he can use to get to you," Randy demanded, "why did you carry our baby inside you for almost nine months."

"Because I couldn't lose..." Sam swallowed the rest.

Randy crossed his arms. He'd wait as long as it took.

He needed to hear the truth, so it would burn through the last of the misguided attachment he felt to her.

"I couldn't lose one more person I cared about," she said. "I fought to keep her. I promised to be careful and stay under the radar from then on. But when that video hit—"

"Video?"

"Of crowds on St. Patrick's Day. The camera zoomed in on me. It was replayed over and over on cable TV. I just happened to catch it flipping channels. It was only a matter of time then... Max said they had to get me to another location, and that things would be even more dicey from now on, and... I had to talk to Gabby, one more time. I couldn't just disappear from her life completely."

Randy felt his outrage slip as more of her story spilled out. He knew firsthand what it was like to have your family ripped away from you. Thinking it was forever. Sam must have been terrified, but she'd still been fighting. Even during the accident her worry had been for the baby she'd put in so much danger. *That* was the woman Randy had thought he'd found again—and lost for good.

"No one would tell me anything except that Gabby was all right." She was rocking the sleeping baby, talking to herself. "I had to know for sure that Gabby was safe."

Which she wasn't.

Clearly, none of them were.

"Sam... What have you gotten me into?"

He crouched in front of her. Instead of demanding to know who Luca was and how long hiding from the man was going to rule their lives, he was leaning closer.

The kiss he wanted, needed, was wrong. She was hurt and confused, and at the moment he didn't exactly have her best interests at heart. But he might never see this woman again. Touch her again.

Damn it! Why did she have to be there making him need the feel of her body against his, while everything she'd said should be making him want to run? Why did she have to be strength and vulnerability? Fear and courage. Illusive, but feeling more solid and real than any other woman he'd ever been with.

The reality of her lips clinging to his instead of shying away destroyed the last of Randy's restraint. Careful of the baby, he slid his palms up her arms while he relearned her touch. Her taste. Her sighs. Her tears…

Tears?

"Stupid…" Sam shook her head and turned her face away. "This is stupid. You have to go. You and the baby, you have to—"

"Shut up." He kissed her again, and then again, until she was kissing back, as desperate as he was. "I'm going, but not before we settle something."

Namely, how she could have slipped so completely beneath the control that had always protected him from this? From feeling so lost at the thought of walking away.

Sam's dark, silky hair was as soft as he remembered. Softer. Her tongue, fluttering against his was every wicked fantasy he'd had since he'd last held her. There was the rightness of kissing fire down her neck. There was the feel of the delicate strength of her back arching into him. All of it, just as he'd remembered it.

His groan swallowed the gasp she couldn't hold back.

"Sam—"

The door from the other room swung open.

"Knock it off." Marshal Dean's deadpan delivery said he wasn't entirely surprised by what he'd barged in on. He waited for Randy to stand and step away. "I assume everyone's on the same page now. Agent North will take the baby while we talk through the relocation plans I've secured approval for."

A female deputy Randy hadn't met yet followed Dean's lead and reached for the baby. Randy planted himself in her path. The woman backed up without comment, her stance relaxed but ready.

"The child's asleep," Dean offered. "She'll be fine in the next room with my people."

"In the next room?" Randy demanded. "Or wherever your people decide to take her once you get her away from me?"

Dean's eyes narrowed. "The baby won't be taken anywhere until the three of us come to an understanding about what happens next. I barely have the manpower to coordinate two security teams. One for Sam. The other for you and your family, Lieutenant Montgomery. A third to take care of a lone child who can no longer remain anonymous is out of the question."

The agent reached around Randy and took his daughter from Sam. Sam's expression was disturbingly blank after the passion Randy had coaxed from her. Almost as if…as if she couldn't feel anything and still be able to let the baby go.

When the deputy disappeared into the other room, Randy rounded on Dean. The marshal was frowning, watching Sam wilt into her pillows.

"What kind of understanding did you have in mind?" Randy asked.

"This was just a visit," Dean reminded him. "I made that clear to you before we got here. You and the baby will be secured with your family just like we discussed."

"That was then." Randy kept his body between the marshal and the mother of his child. "I'm not convinced that's the wisest course of action."

Dean shook his head.

"The first conversation I always have with a protectee," he said, "is about limitations and the importance of controlling your perspective. Sam never accepted that, and the results have been disastrous. Don't make the same mistake she did. Regardless of how…touching the last few minutes have been, I can't keep you three together and keep you safe, if that's what you're about to suggest."

"Safe? You mean the way you've been keeping Sam safe up till now?"

"Federal protectees aren't monitored 24/7, Lieutenant Montgomery. That only happens in TV dramas, at least until my team's dealing with a high-risk situation. Which is what we have now. Sam had a secure identity and 'round-the-clock access to me or one of my deputies if she had a need she couldn't meet herself. It was a textbook relocation until *she* made the decision to exceed the boundaries of her protection, more than once, putting a federal case, her life and now her baby's safety at risk. Are you suggesting that I should have chained her to her bed and stopped her from blowing every safety guideline I gave her? I'm a federal marshal, not a therapist. I can only keep people alive if they aren't hell-bent on getting themselves killed."

"Well, she's not going anywhere now," Randy argued. Sam hadn't moved an inch since Agent North left. She was just sitting there, staring at the door the baby had been taken through. "She can barely stand on her own."

She looked like a broken doll, more and more of the warmth his kiss had brought to her complexion leaking away.

"And you and your child are not an advisable part of Sam's protection going forward," Dean insisted.

"What does separating us now accomplish?"

"For one thing, it would prevent all of you from being taken in one sweep."

"So to simplify your job, she has to stay isolated?" Randy waited for Sam to say something, anything. But she didn't. She wouldn't. She was as good at hiding what she felt as he was. Maybe better.

"I have an injured witness to care for, Lieutenant. Sam needs rest so she's ready to testify whenever the grand jury gets off its ass and calls her up. She's going to be on antibiotics and IV fluids for at least another week. Worrying about a baby would only further exhaust her physical resources, and—"

"Worry?" Sam croaked, finally responding. "You think I'm not going to worry about my daughter just because she's not here? I'm going to worry about her... I'm going to love her and think about her every second of every day for the rest of my life."

"You have to do what's best for the people depending on you." Max stepped closer.

Randy blocked him. "I have a pretty good track record of keeping people safe," he said, not giving himself time to change his mind. He couldn't leave now. Not like this. "I never lose a victim once I'm on the scene. Why don't we make doing the right thing for Sam and her sister and our child my problem from now on? Which means you'll be dealing with me, Marshal Dean, not taking advantage of Sam's fear and confusion. I'm staying."

"What!" Sam gasped.

Uncertainty and pain and betrayal flashed across her face in a jumbled wave. The trust she'd instinctively placed in him at the accident scene was long gone. His anger and accusations had seen to that. The loss of it was like a fist squeezing in Randy's chest.

Max sized Randy up. He glanced at the way Sam was wringing her hands in her lap, then he pulled a cell phone from his pocket and pressed a series of buttons.

"We're ready," he said into the thing.

"Ready for what?" Randy asked.

"I should have listened." Dean headed for the hallway door. "They said this would be your reaction."

"They who?" Randy asked the man's departing back.

PANIC WAS CONSUMING Sam. Panic that she wouldn't have the courage to do the right thing—again.

She never should have held her baby.

Now they'd taken her daughter away. Max would make sure Randy left soon, too. It was what Randy wanted, no matter what he'd said. It was the only way he and the baby would be safe. A man who scaled burning buildings and wielded the Jaws of Life needed to be protected because of Sam—*from* her.

But all Sam could do now was dream of keeping him with her. Standing beside her like he was now, helping her through whatever Max needed her to do next. Protecting their daughter, while Sam got to hold her baby and feed her and cherish her.

Randy had to get out of there. Now. He and the baby had to leave, before Sam lost the ability to watch them go.

"Who are you dragging up here?" Randy asked the new deputy who'd stepped in from the hallway.

"Dragging?" Max actually laughed when he re-entered the room. "It's been all my people could do to keep them from scaling the building to get in here. I'm guessing patience isn't a trait that runs in your family, Lieutenant. This place is like Grand Central, and I'm risking exposure with every second we stand here debating the inevitable. You've got half an hour, than we're all moving."

Before Randy could respond, in walked a beautiful blonde woman and a man that could have been Randy's clone. Only the other guy was even taller and looked even more muscular than Randy, if that was possible. He had to be fire and rescue, too. In fact, if Sam's misfiring memory was correct, he was one of the buddies Randy had been partying with on St. Patrick's Day.

The woman rushed into Randy's embrace.

"Thank God you're okay!" She buried her head against his chest.

He clutched her close and closed his eyes, running a tender hand down her hair. She was obviously someone he cared for deeply. Someone Randy should be spending his time worrying about keeping safe. Someone *not* Sam.

The reality of it stopped Sam's body from tingling in every place his hands had stroked her.

"I'll give you some privacy." She made it to her feet, but she couldn't move.

Her legs refused to hold her up.

She landed back on the cheap mattress with a bounce. She flinched when Randy's arms were there, curling around her and enveloping her with a wave of concern. He'd been ready to be done with her just a few minutes ago. He'd had his say, blamed her for everything that she already knew was her fault, and kissed her out of spite. Now he had to let go.

Because, it hadn't just been spite or retribution or

anger that had passed between them. There had been confused passion, need and surprise muddled together, and finally, a kind of connection that could get him killed.

The other woman knelt beside Randy, her beautiful features clouded with worry.

"Is she okay?" the woman asked.

"She's pretty weak still." Randy took Sam's hand. Sam glared up at him.

"I've been an ass." He moved back. "I've convinced her I'm the enemy."

"Typical." The woman's mouth quirked at the corner.

"I'm not delusional, I know you're not the enemy." Why did they have to make this harder? "You've saved my life. Twice now. Thank you."

The first time, when she'd been on the verge of doing something destructive that night in Savannah. If she hadn't met Randy, who knows where she'd have ended up. Luca's goons might have found her back then and finished this months ago.

"Get away from me," she said to them both. "You're nuts for being anywhere near me."

"I'm here because—" Randy started to say.

"Because you didn't know any better. When you did, you wised up and told me I was on my own. Don't do anything stupid now, Lieutenant. I don't need your death on my hands, too."

Somewhere deep inside, Sam knew she wasn't responsible for the horrible things Luca did. But the guilt of people hurting and dying because of her was never far away. And if clinging to that was the only way she could make herself do what had to be done, so be it.

The blonde glanced between Sam and Randy. A slow smile spread across her face.

"My brother—" she said "—smack dab in the middle of a crisis that's completely out of his control. Well, well, well."

"Brother?" Sam asked.

The resemblance of the other woman to Randy and the man she'd arrived with, despite the differences in their coloring, finally registered.

Randy's sister nodded.

"And there's another hulking mass of testosterone at home with my husband and daughter," she said. "I helped raise the lot of them, and they've always been determined to save the world or die trying. Trust me when I say Montgomery men don't back down when there's a mission to be completed. Mostly because they like to feel in control of the uncontrollable. This one—" she pointed to Randy "—he's never shown a weakness for damsels in distress before." She smiled at Randy then. "She's beautiful. No wonder you haven't been able to forget her."

"I hate to interrupt this charming reunion with something as unimportant as keeping the bunch of you alive," Max said from his post at the door. "But we're down to twenty minutes and there are some tough decisions to make. We all have at least a cursory understanding of the common threat you face. Trust me when I say that the only way Sam, maybe all of you, will survive until the grand jury rules, is for Sam to be isolated again and the rest of you, including the baby, to be secured to separate locations."

"Not going to happen," said the man who looked so much like Randy. "I'm Charlie," he added to Sam.

"Big brother," Randy filled in. "And this is Emma." He nodded toward his sister.

"She's the chief worrier of the pack," Charlie offered. "We were awfully glad to hear that you're alive. You have the most beautiful baby."

We?

"Thank…thank you," Sam stammered.

This wasn't happening.

Charlie's sincerity and Emma's smile and Randy's relief to have his family there had softened his features. A dangerous sense of wanting to belong was grabbing hold of Sam. The Montgomerys, so clearly connected to each other and protective of one another, were the kind of family Sam had always longed to be part of. What she'd hoped to make a reality once she and Gabby started over.

She grabbed her IV stand, pulled herself up from the bed and headed for Max, shrugging off Randy's attempt to stop her. She kept her gaze glued to her federal marshal's.

"I'll check on the baby," she said, "while you get these three to see the reason behind all your rules and regulations. It won't be hard. Randy was ready to toss me out of the window a few minutes ago. Just do a better job of scaring them straight than you did with me. Get them and my daughter out of here."

Randy had a strong, loving family. Of course he

did. That was part of the underlying goodness of the man, no matter the shitty things he'd said to her just now. He cherished the blood ties he was born into. It was no doubt part of what had instinctively attracted her to him. She'd secretly wanted to be someone like him for as long as she could remember.

She would not be the reason Randy lost his family.

Max reached for her. Her glare stalled his hand in midair. Then warmth caressed the arm the doctor had secured in a sling. Sam jumped at the zing of awareness that shot through her from Randy's touch. It was the same need that filled her every time he kissed her.

The need to keep him with her always.

"I'm not going anywhere without you or our daughter," he promised.

"None of us are," Randy's brother agreed. The baby began to cry in the next room, her whimpers deepening the lines bracketing Charlie's frown. "Your child is part of Randy. Part of us. Which makes *you* part of us. No one breaks up our family."

"The situation is too risky—" Max began.

"To secure more than the principal protectee in a single location," Sam finished by rote.

Max nodded. "Especially with the exposure of Lieutenant Montgomery claiming paternity. We couldn't risk someone zeroing in on the dynamic of all of you being in the same place."

"Well, you're just going to have to risk it." Randy pulled Sam and her IV stand closer.

Her resistance fizzled as the room and everyone

in it spun out of focus. Her back curved against Randy's chest. Her head settled beneath his chin. They were a perfect fit.

"You can't…" She turned in his arms, the craving to cling almost overwhelming her. But she'd made enough weak, selfish mistakes. This wasn't her fantasy of being loved and cherished. This was a man who didn't know how to stop playing hero. "I've already ruined your life. Hopefully you can get it back, once this is all over, but—"

"I'm sticking with you through this," he insisted.

"You had it right the first time, Lieutenant, when you were pissed about the danger I've put you all in."

Randy didn't release her. "I *was* pissed. Then shocked about your situation. I jumped to a lot of conclusions. Then I saw you with our baby—"

"A baby that was never supposed to officially exist," Max said. "A daughter that makes you being in complete control of the choices you make out of question until this case is resolved. And even then—"

"I never worry about *then* until I get there," Randy insisted. "I deal with now and only now. That's what saved my sanity when I was five years old, and it's helped me save countless lives since joining the department."

The light was gone from his eyes. Emma and Charlie had tensed as their brother turned back into the closed-off man who'd initially struck out at Sam. Randy stepped away from her. He didn't stop until he was nose to nose with Max.

"You're not going to scare me away from my responsibilities, Marshal Dean. Nothing you could come up with could touch what my family and I have already survived. We'll get through this together. So you can take your scare tactics and shove them up your—"

"Enough, Randy." Charlie's voice was reasonable. But his expression simmered with the same dangerous emotion that Sam felt rolling off his brother. "This isn't about Mom and Dad. Your lady has enough to deal with. Don't add our baggage to it. A child's safety's at stake. A baby you asked me to watch out for, remember?"

"A baby I can't afford to keep with my witness." The *done talking about it* tone of Max's voice ramped up Sam's need to hold her daughter one last time. "It would be too easy a target. My deputies are getting her ready to transport, so—"

"Stop it!" Sam braced herself against the emptiness that was slowly consuming her.

She needed Randy's touch back. Him saying that he wouldn't leave her, even if it wasn't true. She needed her child. And she couldn't let herself have any of it.

"Stop saying my baby has to go!" she shrieked. "We get it. *I* get it! I can't keep my daughter. I can't…"

Suddenly, she was the one in Max's face.

"Why!" she screamed at him. "Why did you bring her here, knowing you were going to rip her away from me again?"

Each word was shaking, sobbing proof that Sam couldn't do this. She'd never been strong enough to do any of it. She sank to her knees, her arms wrapped around herself, hating the numbness that was taking over.

Then there was warmth behind her. Following her down. Enveloping her, so she wasn't alone. He whispered soft, soothing sounds into her ear. Sounds that insisted this could still be all right. That she didn't have to be strong enough on her own. She just had to hold onto him until the hopelessness inside her stopped screaming to give up.

"Shh…" Randy said. "We'll find some way through this."

"We?" She clung to the word. To Randy.

"We." He held her a little tighter.

"Touching," Max commented.

Sam glared up at him.

Her unflappable federal marshal looked unsure for the first time she could remember. Concerned. He checked his watch.

"You can't keep her right now, Sam." There was compassion in his statement, but no room for debate.

"Then tell me how I'm going to live without her." It was the same thing she'd said about Gabby, when Max had first relocated Sam. She'd been promised they would only be apart for a few months. "I can't do this anymore."

"It's just a little longer," Max reasoned. "Then—"

"Then there will be some other judicial delay. Luca has the money and connections to tie the case up forever. Which means I'll never be free. I'll never get Gabby out. I'll never see my baby again.

That's what he wants." Sam shuddered. "He wants to take away everything, and Luca always gets what he wants…."

She was ranting. Weak. Losing it. She had to pull it together. She had to keep moving. To remember that Randy had hated her when she'd first told him about the case and the danger she'd forced on him. So what if he'd kissed her and was having a flash of momentary guilt over his threat to rip their child from her arms? All that mattered was protecting their daughter.

Randy would blame Sam if he stayed, despise her even more when everything went to hell again. There was no future for them.

"Shh," Randy soothed. "You're safe. Our daughter's safe."

"No," Sam said. "She's not."

Sam got to her feet with Randy's help, then she edged away.

"You agreed to the terms of your protection." Max actually sounded sorry. "You've run rogue twice already. I won't cover for you again. This detail was already costing the federal government a fortune. It's now doubled in size. Three strikes, and you're out, kid. Stick to the deal you made, or—"

"Or what?" she snapped.

"I know it's a bad situation—"

"Bad? I've run from a goon who lied to me every day of my life, and as a reward I moved on to your doublespeak. What's the difference? I'm still trapped."

"I'm not the bad guy here," Max said.

"No…" Sam closed her eyes.

It wasn't his fault that she'd never let herself trust Max or any of his deputies. She'd never really trusted anybody except Luca—a long time ago, back when he'd seemed like her knight in shining armor.

"It's no one's fault I have to walk away from my child now," she admitted, "but mine."

"There has to be another way," Randy insisted.

She finally looked up at him—a new knight who wanted her to believe he could make the loneliness go away. "You have to go with our baby. I have to go with Max. Everyone has to be safe."

"No matter what that does to you?" Randy cupped her cheek. "I was angry. For a few minutes all I could see was what this is doing to me and my life. But when I really looked into your eyes... This is killing you, Sam. There has to be another way."

"How about a compromise?" a rough voice intruded.

"What?" Sam asked Charlie.

"You can't keep your baby, but you're clearly not well enough to get through a separation like this alone." Charlie's gaze switched to Max and grew cold. "You can only cover two protection teams. Why does that have to mean Sam goes back to dealing with this on her own?"

Randy was nodding. Smiling. Confronting Max himself.

"My family will take the baby with them," he said. "But I'm staying with Sam."

"No," Max said. "Out of the question."

"Then your plan must be to drive Sam into a nervous breakdown." Charlie tugged his sister to his side. "Look at what this is doing to the witness you need rested and ready to testify in federal court. Let my brother help Sam, and maybe you've got a shot at nailing this Luca character."

"I have a teenager to help look after the baby," Emma assured Sam, "and a husband who loves kids and is the poster boy for protecting and serving. Your daughter will be safe." She glanced toward Max. "And you won't have any problems with us abiding by your protection guidelines."

"We're well aware of your husband's connections with state and federal agencies, Mrs. Downing." Max didn't sound reassured. "The good detective digging into Sam's situation wasn't a wise move."

"He'll make sure the rest of us toe the line from here on out," Emma insisted. "Rick was ready to wring my neck for insisting to see my brother. You want that baby hidden for as long as you need her to be? You want Sam calm enough to be of any use to you?" Emma blasted Sam with cat-green eyes that were alive with her brother's intelligence and determination. "Leave the baby with me, and Randy with the woman he's determined to help."

Sam realized her hand had somehow found its way into Randy's grasp.

"Chris and I will be there, too," Charlie promised her. "You don't have to worry. My brothers and sister and I were separated as children. Emma fought to get us all back. Our family stays together." He nodded toward the infant sounds still coming from the other room. "All of our family."

Family…

Randy's free hand cupped her cheek. "Trust them. Trust me, Sam, before you lose everything."

"Trust?" She choked on the word.

Max stared at them all with the eye of a gambler weighing his odds.

The baby started crying in earnest.

Sam slipped away from the living nightmare, leaving Max to do his dirty work. No way would he cave to the Montgomerys' demands. And Sam had to see her daughter one last time before she was gone.

In the adjoining room, Glinda glanced over Sam's shoulder before handing over the baby. Then she and another deputy Sam didn't know left.

She snuggled her daughter's wriggling body close, sensing someone behind her. She knew somehow that it was Max who'd followed her, even though she desperately wanted it to be Randy. She turned to watch Max close the door on the conversation in the other room.

"I am sorry you can't keep her," he said.

"I don't have a choice. You've made that clear."

"About the baby, no. About trusting her father to help you—"

"Don't tell me you actually think Randy should stay with me!"

"You're exhausted and emotionally drained. If having Montgomery around is what's best for you, if he's willing to risk—"

"Like Peter was willing to risk his life to stay with me?"

Sam's fiancé had been blinded by his need to protect her, too. She could still see Peter's smile as he'd promised to love her and take care of her forever. Then her memory fast-forwarded to an image of him bleeding to death, his head still on the pillow they'd shared, his eyes open, staring up at her.

Luca's explanation for the killing?

He'd been doing what was best for Sam. What was best for the family.

"My other team will keep the Montgomerys and your daughter safe," Max promised. "No one will be looking their way. They're a good family. They're—"

"They're better than anything I could have dreamed up for my child." Sam kissed her daughter's head, fighting more useless tears.

"It will only be for a few more weeks," Max promised. "The prosecutor is pushing the judge to lock down the grand jury. Once this is over, you and your baby—"

"No." Sam handed over the baby she couldn't bring herself to name.

It was time to face reality. This wasn't about her guilt over Peter, or her fear of what Randy might come to mean to her if he didn't leave. This was about a baby, a new life. A new chance she'd sacrifice anything to see come true. Even her own heart.

"She's Randy's baby," she said as Max gazed down at her daughter. "The Montgomery family is where she belongs. Just look at how they've pulled together, and they've had only a few days to process all of this. My daughter should be with them when this is over, not running to God knows where and pretending to be someone else. Letting the Montgomerys raise her is the only way this will ever be right."

Max's head snapped up. "What did you say?"

Sam hugged her injured arm and turned away. "Luca's never going to stop, Max. It'll be him or someone he sends, hunting me for the rest of my life. The prosecutor made that clear from day one. They could keep coming forever. Gabby's already a part of it, but I won't put a baby through this. Never feeling safe. Never being free of it. Place her with the Montgomerys. Permanently. The federal prosecutor will know what kind of paperwork needs to be filed. Send Randy back with them tonight. Make sure he never finds me again. Do that, and I'll be a good girl from now on."

"You…you can't be serious."

"Do it, or I'll run again the first chance I get. I won't put my daughter in any more danger than I already have. Keep her away from me."

There was a long pause. Followed by the door to the other room opening with a soft whoosh that sounded like Sam's last hope slipping away. But Max's agreement meant there was still a chance for her daughter to be free of this. Somehow that was going to have to be enough.

Sam could hear quiet discussion, as if the Montgomerys were too stunned by her decision to manage anything louder. Randy's voice raised once. Just once. Then there was only silence, followed by the sound of another door opening and closing—the one to the hallway beyond the other room.

Randy and his family were on their way. They'd be safe now.

It seemed like forever before Max's footsteps approached.

"So where to now?" Sam wiped at the tears she'd finally let fall. She couldn't face him yet, but it was time to face the commitment she'd made. "No more coloring outside the lines, I swear. Keep my child and her father safe, and I'll be a model protectee from now on."

"That's good to hear," said the last voice she expected to hear.

Sam spun around so fast, she clung to her IV stand for balance.

"Randy?" He filled the doorway, all strength and determination that made her heart hurt with something too close to hope.

"But why don't we agree," he continued, "that our daughter's father can take care of himself, and move on to worrying about her mother?"

A sob escaped Sam. A flood of disbelief that left her shaking. Before she knew it, Randy had pulled her into the safety of his arms.

How could he still be there?

After everything she'd said, she was right where she needed to be—in his arms. He tipped her face up. His expression was wary, giving nothing away. But his thumb wiped at the tears streaming down her cheeks.

"Don't…" she begged.

He kissed her words away, and she couldn't keep

her lips from clinging, or her heart from needing this to *really be real*. That's what Gabby had always called their dream of a family that felt on the inside what it appeared on the outside. Close. Tight. Safe. Never-ending.

But Sam had to remember that Randy was merely a man determined to protect and serve. Not a lover losing his heart the way she was. He was doing the right thing for his child.

This wasn't a forever thing.

It could only end bloody for her.

But there was no stopping the secret desire bubbling up.

"Don't leave me, Randy. Please…"

RANDY HAD ALWAYS THOUGHT Emma was the most amazing woman he'd ever met. She'd sacrificed her childhood to keep their family together.

But Sam… She'd intended to send her baby away. For good, her federal marshal had said. She'd been willing to give up the daughter who clearly meant everything to her, because she was convinced it was the only way to keep the child safe. In no small part because Randy had unloaded on her and made her out to be responsible for everything that had happened.

What had that decision cost her?

This wasn't the first time she'd tried to slip away.

Leaving him in Savannah hadn't been a rejection. It had been about protecting him, just like she was trying to protect their daughter now. But he'd seen her face when she'd looked down at her child. They all had. Telling Dean to give her baby away must have killed her, but she'd done what she'd thought she had to.

That kind of strength and courage was a beauty that went deeper than Sam's sweet face. It was the essence of the woman in his arms—the same woman he hadn't been able to stay clear of in Savannah.

"I'm not going anywhere." He kissed her, trying to reassure her with touch.

Sam shook her head, rejecting the promise he had no right to make after the way he'd behaved. Randy held on tighter, careful of her injuries but determined to get through.

She didn't need to protect herself from him. Not now. Not ever. And he didn't care how many of Dean's agents wandered in the room to witness his claim.

When Sam wilted against him and welcomed his deepening touch, Randy accepted that what he needed from her went far beyond earning her trust. Because no matter how much he'd let Sam down, she clearly craved this, too. This closeness. This bizarre knowing that they somehow belonged together, no matter how little time they had.

Sam held on tighter, as if she couldn't feel enough of him. Her unspoken need drove his higher, until she pulled away.

"We can't." She looked to the other room. "Max…"

"They're giving us some time before we have to go." Randy backed them into the half-open door, shutting it the rest of the way. He gently leaned her against it, then covered Sam's body with his. "Max's worried—"

"—about his protection detail." She shied away from Randy's next kiss.

"He's worried about you." Randy caught her face in his palms and kissed the bruise beneath her right eye. Then her nose. Her mouth. When her eyes closed, he kissed each lid. "*I'm* worried about you. You're running on adrenaline, Sam. You're being forced to make life and death decisions that are ripping your heart out. You shouldn't even be out of the hospital."

"It…" Her voice had deepened to a husky timbre. "I'm doing what's best for the baby. For your family."

"But not for you."

Randy nipped her neck just below her ear, where he remembered she liked it. Sam's legs buckled. She'd have fallen, but his palm cupped the softness of her bottom. Nestled it tighter against him. Need surged in a dizzying rush.

"Forget every stupid thing I said before," he said. "Forget everything except that I'm here, and I'm not going anywhere. Stop running, Sam. Slow down long enough to choose what's best for *you*. Let me help you do that."

She was staring at him as if she'd never seen him before. Never felt what he was making her feel. It was the same expression he'd seen on her face during those unguarded hours in March. It had intrigued him then. Now, the lost emptiness in her gaze broke his heart.

"Sam…"

She was staring at his mouth like an addict craving her next fix.

Don't leave me, Randy...

His lips found hers in the most important kiss of his life. Sam's fingers clenched in his shirt, then flattened across his chest, then dug in again as passion rushed through them. She was half his size and weak as a kitten. But the strength of her need was the same as last spring—when she'd trusted and let go and become a living fire in his arms, no matter how much danger she'd been in even then.

"That's right." The memory of the touch and taste of her flooded him. "I'm here, baby. I'm not going anywhere. This is real, Sam. Trust it. No one, not even this Luca of yours, is going to get to you while I'm here."

Sam tensed, her eyes fluttering open.

"Shh..." Randy cursed himself for ruining the moment. He smoothed his hand down the delicate curves motherhood had added to her body. He rested his forehead against hers. "I'm sorry. For all of this. For everything you've been through. For making it worse, because—"

"It... It's not your fault."

"None of this is *your* fault, either." Randy sighed when she shook her head. "You're hell-bent on protecting a newborn life, a sister, me and my family. Half of us you've barely met, but you're going to protect us. And damn it, if that kind of bravery doesn't make it impossible for me to do anything but want to kiss you again."

Sam licked her lower lip, torturing him.

"But you said…" She shook her head instead of continuing. "You don't understand—"

"I understand all I have to for now. Just—"

"No, you don't. There are things you can't know—"

"The only things I care about are you and our child."

"A child you took home with you but never named?" Her stare held his.

"I…" Why hadn't he even thought of naming the baby? "It's just that she never really seemed real, until I saw her in your arms. Then—"

"It's okay." Sam's smile was brittle, but she made it stick. "I understand. I couldn't name her, either. It would make what I knew I had to do harder. But you and your family… You'll have plenty of time for that, once I'm out of the picture. You'll be free to—"

"You're not out of the picture." He'd told Dean he'd handle this. That he'd make Sam see reason.

"After the trial, I—"

"You'll be naming your daughter yourself, once we're sure you're both safe."

"She's your daughter now. You said so yourself."

"She's *our* daughter. I was talking stupid when I first got here. Don't for a minute think that—"

"Think what? That I don't belong with you and your cozy family? You were right. Everything you said about me and this insanity was right on. You let me see her. H-hold her. Now get away from me. Whatever responsibility you feel toward me, get over it. Protect our daughter and your family from the darkness I've brought into your life. That's all you owe me."

"And walking away from us—our baby and me and my brothers and sister when they're willing to stand by you—walking away from what you need is your only option? Is that what you want me to believe?"

"What exactly do you think I need?" She grew rigid in his arms. "Who are you to tell me what to think and feel, besides someone who looked like he wanted to spit on me not long after discovering that I was still alive. What? You suddenly think you have the answer to all my problems now, just because you feel guilty for being an asshole?"

"Maybe I'm someone who wants you to have a future, instead of this insane half life you seem resigned to live."

Randy blinked, as stunned as Sam seemed by what he'd just said. Until that moment, thoughts of the future—*their* future—hadn't been part of the deal. At least not consciously.

But thinking of Sam and their daughter starting over somewhere else, away from him…

"A future?" Sam yanked away as if he'd slapped her, leaving his body aching to feel hers close again. "The only future I have is—"

The boom of an explosion obliterated the rest of her tirade.

The room shook. The floor shuddered beneath them. Sam screamed and lost her balance.

"I've got you!" Randy caught her and pulled them both to the ground, rolling so that Sam landed on top.

Her IV stand crashed down beside them.

The lights flickered, then went out.

"What…?" Sam gasped. "What was that?"

"I don't know." The building was still shaking. "Lie still and let me check you out."

Basic medical training took over. He searched blindly until he found her IV. The needle was still in place. His hands fluttered firmly but gently down her body. No sign of injuries to her arms, legs or ribs. Only then did Randy pull them both up until they were sitting. He tucked Sam to his side and tried to calm his own breathing.

Alarms sounded.

The sprinklers sputtered to life, raining freezing water down on them.

"Fire!" Sam shrank against him.

"Not necessarily." But… "Max and his men— where are they? They should be posted outside every door, even if some of them left with my family."

Charlie and Emma.

The baby.

Were they gone? Were they still in the building? God, what if they hadn't made it out? What if they'd been caught up in some sort of attempt to get to Sam?

"Luca!" Sam began to struggle against Randy. "He's found me."

"Hold still." Randy pulled her head back to his shoulder.

He ran a soothing hand down her soggy hair. She was shivering. He grabbed the spread off one of the room's double beds and dragged it around her to help shield her from the water. Then he tugged the IV stand closer and detached her bag of saline and whatever else they were giving her.

"We have to get out of here!" she gasped.

"We have to sit tight and wait. Let's give the feds another minute, before—"

"What if there's no one coming for us?"

"We're going to stay calm. Panic's only going to make things worse."

Rule number one when running into a fire—see danger as a worthy adversary, *not* as sure and sudden death. Respect it. Outsmart it. But never give in to the fear of it.

"We're waiting here until—" he began to say.

The door to the hallway burst open, ushering in a cloud of dark smoke. Randy could barely see through the scant light filtering through from the room's shaded windows. He shoved Sam to the floor, preparing to throw himself over the bed at whomever might be approaching.

"What's happening?" Sam whispered.

"Stay down."

Randy stared toward the door. Listened. There was nothing but the blare of the fire alarm. Then came a distant, angry growl Randy knew all too well.

A growing fire.

They were trapped. Running for safety might be exactly what whomever had caused the explosion wanted—assuming it had been set intentionally. But staying there waiting to be burned alive was a death sentence.

Where were the damned marshals?

"I'll be right back." He caressed Sam's cheek in the darkness.

"No!" She grabbed his arm. "Luca will kill you!"

"I have to—"

"Sam? Montgomery?" came a shout from the hallway.

"Dean?" Randy half carried Sam as he helped her crawl through the thickening smoke toward the shadowy figure now kneeling in the doorway. "What the hell's going on?"

"They've blown the elevators," Dean answered. "Fire's already filling the floors below us, where the charges were detonated. My team's isolated the intruders. This floor's secure. But the stairwell's our only exit. Are you certified with a handgun?"

Randy couldn't focus on a single word the other man had said. Because while Dean had been talking and the alarms had been blaring and the heat of the fire had been rolling closer, Sam's marshal had pressed an automatic weapon into Randy's hand. Randy's fingers wrapped around the grip, his past creeping closer than it had since he'd been a child.

"Montgomery!" Dean demanded when Randy didn't respond.

"I certified fifteen years ago." Randy had made a point of it. As a teenager. Long before joining the fire department. He'd learned how to build, dismantle, arm, disarm, clean and store a variety of guns. All illegally. All before he'd graduated middle school. Then he'd made Emma promise never to keep a gun in their home.

"You okay, Sam?" Dean asked.

"Yes." The answer was shaky, followed by a cough that ripped Randy securely back to the present.

"Let's get you out of here." He checked the gun's safety, then secured it at his back in the waistband of his jeans. "Stairs are to the left," he said to Dean. "Four doors to the end of the hallway, on the right." It was instinct, cataloging floor plan details wherever he went. "Stay below the smoke line, where the air is still breathable."

Sam's marshal nodded and turned down the hall, hustling in a crouch.

"We'll be out of this before you know it," Randy assured Sam. He was protecting her from this, even if she refused to trust him with anything else.

She tried to crawl and cried in pain, her shoulder giving out. A shuddering cough consumed her. Suddenly he was the one who was close to losing it— because he couldn't lose *her*. He lifted her slight frame against his body in a hold that resembled a football carry.

"I can't…" Her body drooped in his grasp. "I just ca—"

"I'm going to slip you onto my back, baby." Randy forced confidence into his voice. "It's going to hurt your shoulder. I'm sorry. But it'll get us down the hall and the stairs. All you have to do is trust me and relax. You can do that, right?"

Not giving her time to think, Randy tucked her IV bag into his belt, slid her right arm around his back, angled his shoulder beneath her and lifted as he twisted, pulled and rose to his knees. Sam slid onto his back with a squeal of pain, then struggled when she almost slid off the other side.

"Relax, baby." Randy captured her with his right arm, plastering her to his back while he used his left hand to crawl after Dean. "I do this every day."

But never before with so precious a burden.

"You okay?"

He took her non-answer as a positive sign while he brushed against the outer wall of each room they passed, feeling for any heat transferring from a fire that might be building inside. He counted the doorways they had to pass until they reached the stairs, his internal map leading the way through the swelling darkness. Smoke was rising, swallowing everything.

He squinted against the fire's toxic vapors.

"How's the pain, baby? You still with me?"

Another stream of coughing told him she was at least conscious. He didn't let himself stop and check her condition. A second's delay could mean the difference between them getting off the floor, or not.

"Hang in there, sweetheart."

She couldn't seem to catch her breath. Each painful cough was killing him as he reached the final doorway and turned toward where the stairwell should be. Her thin arm wrapped around his neck, squeezing trustingly.

Adrenaline rushed through Randy. A new determination to get Sam out alive. He collided with a body he hadn't seen kneeling in front of him.

Max rose to his feet.

"Ready?" the other man yelled over the blaring alarm.

"Wait!" Randy stood, bringing Sam with him.

He cringed, feeling her flinch in pain. But he felt the metal fire door, anyway. The metal was lukewarm to the touch.

"Go!" he shouted to Dean. Then to Sam, he said, "Hang on to me, baby. Three flights down, and we're out."

"Be ready." Dean pushed through the door and led the way into the stairwell's dimness. The marshal's gun was up, aligned with a flashlight Randy could now see through the cleaner air around them. "We'll stop three steps before each landing. Wait until I give the all clear. My people are securing the exit route, but we can't be too careful. Follow my lead."

Randy followed, keeping Sam on his back. He stayed bent at an angle that would keep her balanced there, trying to cause her as little pain as possible. She silently endured, but the arm locked around his neck was ice cold. She needed to be lying down. Was her IV still inserted? What if there was someone waiting on the stairs to pick them off while they fled?

He felt the imprint of the gun Dean had given him. He accepted the sudden conviction of knowing that he'd use it if he had to. Whoever this Luca was, he knew Sam was alive, partially because of Randy's actions. And the goon was still gunning for her. Randy wasn't letting him anywhere near Sam.

They paused at the first landing. There was a

marshal posted at that door. Dean and his man swept the next flight of stairs before continuing. The same pattern was repeated at the next door, their group growing with each flight.

It was taking too damn long. Sam was shivering now. Finally, the reassuring clamor of sirens drew closer. Dean, Randy, Sam and the three other agents they'd collected burst outside, into an alley.

A utility van was waiting, doors open. Randy swung Sam into his arms. Her eyes were closed. She was out cold. They were hustled into the van. Bodies crowded in around them. The doors swung shut, and they were off.

CHAPTER TEN

CHARLIE WASN'T LIKING a word he was hearing of the clipped conversation going on between Glinda and whoever she had on the phone—one of the marshals who'd stayed behind with Randy and Sam at the hotel. What he liked less was that no one was communicating a thing to him and Emma.

Glinda and the SUV's driver had been all business. No explanation of their destination as they blew out of Atlanta midtown with unmarked sedans leading and following. No ETA for when they'd arrive wherever, or if Chris or Rick and Jessie would already be waiting there. Except something at the hotel had clearly gone wrong only minutes after they'd left.

Glinda's body was tense as she talked into the hands-free device wrapped around her ear. The driver listened on an identical device while Charlie held his sister's hand, their arms lying across the top of their niece's car seat. Emma alternated between staring out the window and staring at the baby. Her husband put his life on the line every day, the same as Charlie and Randy and Chris did. Emma dealt with worry as a way of life. But when Glinda once again said, "Understood," into her hands-free, Emma clutched Charlie's hand tighter.

"What do you think's happening back there?" She never cried, not in front of the brothers she'd raised from boys to hulking men. But moisture was pooling in her eyes now.

"It's going to be okay," he assured her.

Emma nodded and bent to gently kiss the baby who'd had another bottle and fallen into a post-snack stupor.

"Randy's a big boy," Charlie insisted, hoping he'd done the right thing by suggesting this setup. "He's in good hands."

"He's in love." Emma was back to staring out the window. "And he doesn't know it yet. At least he's nowhere ready to deal with it. He's so focused and controlled, but I know him, Charlie. He doesn't trust his feelings. He'll be fighting the attachment, while he feels responsible for the woman, while someone's trying to shut her up for good… Why won't they tell us what's going on!"

The baby stiffened at Emma's raised voice and gave an annoyed warble, threatening full-fledged wailing if they didn't keep it down. Glinda shifted in her seat. She glanced into the backseat. Emma stared daggers at the other woman, daring her to not fill them in.

"Our team intercepted a strike at the hotel," the deputy finally explained. "It's contained. Your brother's safe."

"A strike?" Emma gasped.

"A charge was planted in the elevator shaft. It activated, but—"

"The hotel was bombed?" Charlie's fingers clenched around his sister's. "But everyone got out, right?"

"There was a fire. Your brother piggybacked Sam down the stairs with our team covering. They're en route to a secure location."

"But?" he asked.

She hadn't answered his question.

Glinda turned back to the windshield. "But we lost two agents on the scene. They took out the guys booby-trapping the elevator, but they were caught in the blast."

Charlie sat back. Randy and Sam had been attacked only minutes after Charlie had walked away from his baby brother.

It registered that Emma hadn't said anything after Glinda's revelation. Charlie inhaled, determined to reassure her, somehow. But when he looked at his sister, his stomach dropped.

"What?"

Emma let go of his hand and struggled to unbuckle the baby seat's restraints. She snatched the little girl to her shoulder, patting her back.

"What!" Charlie had never seen Emma this freaked.

"I don't think she's breathing." His sister switched the baby to her lap and rubbed her hand over the newborn's tiny chest. "Her lips are turning blue. She's not breathing!"

CHAPTER ELEVEN

"I NEED TO TALK with Max." Sam didn't let herself look at Randy, even if she couldn't let go of his hand.

They'd almost died.

The world had stopped spinning about half an hour ago. That made her a coward to still be lying on their new room's bed, her eyes closed, clinging to Randy.

"You need to rest," Randy insisted. "The way the doctor told you to."

Randy had been quiet since they'd reached the SUV. He hadn't demanded to know more about her life in New York. Not on the long ride to the new location, which turned out to be a lodge a hundred miles away and in the North Georgia mountains. Not while Sam had been checked out by the doctor who'd been waiting for them. Not even after Sam and Randy had been left to wash off the damp stench of smoke and fear that had followed them from the explosion.

But he hadn't let Sam out of his sight, either, except when she'd taken her turn in the shower. And she'd had the strong suspicion after catching the hooded determination in his eyes when she'd emerged and slid onto the bed, that he'd been contemplating following her into the bathroom if she hadn't come out when she did.

There was a lot behind that sharp gaze—the intensity of a man watching, waiting, looking for an excuse to pounce. He was angry again, and he should be. He was terrified for his family and their baby. So was she. Now, all she had to do was convince herself to let go.

Nothing we can do now but wait, Randy said after she'd woken up in the SUV—the only other time he'd said anything at all. They'd just been told that his family and the baby were clear. *They got everyone out alive. That's what's important.*

He'd sounded reassuring enough. Except then they'd heard that two of Max's people had died protecting them. And no matter where they hid Sam next, the danger would keep coming. Luca would eventually find her.

"Go get Max for me." Sam tried to sit up, but dizziness sent her back to the mattress.

Just a few more minutes.

That's all she needed.

"He's debriefing his team." Randy's fingers stayed wrapped around hers. "What's the rush?"

"Because I can't take this anymore." She really couldn't. "We both know you're going to go. Just have your say and get on with it!"

He inhaled.

Slowly.

He didn't budge an inch.

Sam sat, somehow, and scooted to the other side of the bed—as far as her new IV would allow. Pillows bunched behind her, softening her body's contact with the headboard.

"Stop playing whatever game you're playing—" her voice rose "—and just let me have it!"

He blinked, his expression wary.

"Why don't you tell me what I'm supposed to be playing at," he said.

"Being a good guy, no matter how pissed you are. Being the guy that does the *right* thing, that fixes whatever needs to be fixed, no matter how much danger is involved. In case you hadn't noticed, there's a team of this country's finest buzzing around me. I'm all full up with responsible, dependable heroes. You're officially off the hook here, Lieutenant Montgomery."

His stare grew even more intense. "And if I'm not looking to be let off the hook?"

"Someone just tried to blow you up. Now beat it. This has nothing to do with you."

It couldn't.

"But it has everything to do with you," he reasoned, insufferably calm. "Which means it has everything to do with my child. Doesn't that give me a right to care what happens to you?"

"Our baby. Exactly!" A wave of need hit Sam. What wouldn't she give to be holding her daughter again? To hear the peaceful, sleepy sounds she'd made. "You should be with her."

"Now we're back to this being all about the baby." Randy's anger finally broke free. "Is that really the best you've got?"

"What I've *got* is a dead fiancé and a car crash and

buildings exploding and burning around me. Are you really that stupid?"

"Is that what kissing me back at the hotel felt like?" Randy pushed off the bed, but instead of heading for the door he bent and braced his hands on either side of Sam. "Stupid?"

"That's exactly what it was, you idiot." The words sliced at Sam, while she watched them work their damage on Randy.

Frustration clouded his features, then hurt. Then his expression cooled into the kind of cynical acceptance that shouldn't be possible in a man who cared for things so deeply. He straightened and sank his hands into the back pockets of the jeans someone had found for him. He settled back on his heels, staring at the carpet.

Sam suspected he was counting to ten.

Okay, maybe twenty.

"Maybe I am an idiot," he finally said. "My whole life, I've avoided shit like this. Relationships aren't for me. I've known it since I was a kid. Trusting isn't my thing. It's genetic, I suppose. So I stayed clear of women who wanted more than a nice ride or two, or a few fun weeks."

When Randy looked up, a part of him wasn't there anymore. She could feel the shift as well as see it. Something had disappeared inward, traveling to the same damaged place she'd sensed when they'd grown quiet after making love. He'd stared into her eyes then, as if she was the first woman he'd let himself really see. The first heart he'd somehow known would understand what was beating inside him. That was the moment Sam had fallen in love with him.

Now she was falling all over again.

"So tell me why I can't protect myself from you?" he asked. "Why I was careless and made a baby with you. Why did just talking with you while my crew cut you out of your car feel like coming home—even though my heart was breaking for what you were going through? Why did our daughter become the most important thing in my life, the moment I set eyes on her—no matter how hard it was for me to accept that I was a father? It's not just responsibility or duty. I'm still here because I can't be anywhere else, Sam. I'm not just some guy feeling responsible. And I'm not oblivious to the danger surrounding us. I'm angry and I'm confused and I'm worried about everyone I care about. But I'm still here. I can't be anywhere else. Meanwhile you're determined to get rid of me as fast as you can, and every tie to me—even your own daughter."

The loneliness in his voice, the loss…

He was no longer the untouchable man he showed the world. This was whatever had formed Randy. Whatever tragedy had left Emma to raise her brothers.

Sam realized her hand was reaching toward him. She needed to take back every hurt she'd caused, every pain she hadn't soothed. This man was her daughter's future. It was dangerous for Sam to see a place for herself there. But he was making it impossible not to.

When Randy's fingers tangled with hers, she

tugged him closer. Back to her side where she'd needed him all along.

"I don't want to get rid of you." Her eyes stung from how good it felt to lean against him. "That's why I need you to do the right thing. It's not fair, but you have to be the grownup here, Randy. Nothing can happen to you I need... Our daughter needs you."

He brushed the bangs out of her eyes. His touch was soothing and safe. Perfect.

"What do you need, baby?" he asked, catching her slip. "I've known a lot of women in my life. Enough to think I'd seen every way you can try to hook a man who's immune to being hooked. But this is the first time I've met a woman more desperate to stay immune than I am."

"I..."

Maybe they were the same. Both running from the past. Both going nowhere. Maybe that's part of what she'd felt in Savannah, and every moment they'd spent together the last few days.

"I want you and our daughter to be safe," she made herself say.

"We'll all be safe." He tipped her face up until she could see the worry in his warm brown eyes. "But not if you disappear from your child's life, when you clearly care for her. She belongs with you, Sam. Let me help you fight to make that happen."

The way another man had promised to fight with her.

She shook her head. "If you knew the whole story, you'd see..."

A story she wasn't supposed to reveal the details

of. Max had made that clear when they'd arrived at the new safe house. Giving Randy or his family more information might compromise the prosecution's case. Luca might walk.

"I have my own past." Randy kissed her forehead. Sam closed her eyes and drank in the caress. "I may not be being chased by a maniac, but I know what evil is. I watched it destroy my family. I watched him kill my mother. Whatever you're mixed up in, I don't for a second believe it's your fault, no matter what I said before. And I won't let it rip you away from your daughter. I know firsthand what that can do to a kid."

"Him?" Sam tried to focus on what Randy was saying. To keep her lips from finding the sensitive skin along the column of his neck, just where she knew a kiss would send his entire body into shivers.

Evil had killed his mother?

His touch was calling to her. His heartbreaking revelation echoed through her mind. Someone had killed his mother?

Maybe they were the same...

"Who?" she asked. "Randy, who killed—"

"It doesn't matter." He leaned into her touch, the sexual energy between them sparking. Heating up.

"But..." She tried to hold back her next kiss, but her teeth found his earlobe and nipped softly, then harder when he groaned in approval.

"Don't you see?" he asked as she stared up into his stormy eyes. "Nothing matters right now but this. You—trusting me enough to let me help get you back to our daughter. You trusting us, the way you did in the accident, in Savannah…"

"Us? This is just…" What? What were they doing? "It's not real."

There was no *us*.

He laid her back on the bed. He gently removed the sling from her arm. His body followed her down until he'd covered her with the promise that nothing would ever feel as good as the sensation of Randy surrounding her, loving her, protecting her.

"Tell me you really want me to go, Sam. Make me throw you away, the way I have everyone else besides my family. Tell me this isn't real enough to fight for, and I'll leave."

RANDY HAD NEVER let the memories this close. He'd left the lost, angry child he'd been behind years ago. Now, the attack at the hotel and the very real possibility of never seeing Sam again were bringing it all back.

She was serious. She wanted him gone, and it wasn't just about wanting him to protect their daughter. Sam was trying to protect him. She really believed there was no other option but to face this maniac Luca alone.

But Randy had her beside him now. Beneath him. Holding on to him as if he was her lifeline. As if she'd found someone she could trust with her secrets, the way Randy was certain he could trust her. Hearing her sigh in pleasure pushed his dark memories away. It made him even more determined to fight, to hold on, instead of letting go.

Nothing had been real before now. No other woman had fit against him so perfectly. Wherever she'd come from, whoever this Luca was, Randy knew exactly what that world had done to Sam. But the answer wasn't Sam giving her daughter away or giving up on him.

Her lips were like tiny, stinging butterflies fluttering against his skin, down his neck to just above the collar of his T-shirt. His fingers tangled in her hair and held her head in place, a silent plea for her to continue.

"Tell me you don't want this," he challenged.

"This…" She shook her head. Her hand traced fire down his spine, urging his hips closer. "It's just a dream…"

Randy rocked against her. Gentle. He had to be gentle.

"Prove it." His touch cherished her tucked-in waist. The curve of her belly. "Show me how it's not real."

Sam wasn't like the other women he'd been to bed with. She wasn't just one night. Since their time together in Savannah, she'd become a part of him. His past and his future. He needed her both places. He needed her, period.

He pushed away long enough to walk to the closed door and lock it. He pulled the T-shirt off on his way back. Then he stood there, watching her watch him with so much fear and confusion in her expression, she looked as if she might shatter. But this was Sam. A survivor. He doubted there was anything she couldn't handle. Even accepting him as part of her fight, instead of someone else to run from.

She was wearing a flowing, blue cotton dress, with a long skirt and sleeves. Buttons from the collar all the way down to the hem. It covered nearly every inch of her.

Randy knelt on the bed, watching her closely as he reached to undo the first button. Then the second. His body was screaming to take more. He gently smoothed the backs of his fingers over the skin he'd revealed. The softness, the heat, the thundering of Sam's pulse stopped him. He wanted to savor all of it.

He bent, nuzzling the sensitive curve of her breast. He drank in the resulting catch in her breath. She was hard and soft and capable and vulnerable. He wanted her skin, her body, her mind, her heart.

"How did this happen?" He worked the rest of the buttons free. "How did you become something I can't resist?"

She shook her head. Not to say no, because her hands were unfastening his belt and then the snap and zipper on his jeans.

"How can you get to me this way?" He undid the last button on her dress and spread the soft cotton open.

Sam wore nothing beneath. A soft cry of distress was his only warning before she tried to cover herself with her hands. He pushed her arms to the mattress and ran his tongue between her breasts, down to her delicate belly button.

"You're sweet," he whispered, determined to show her how *real* his feelings were, even if he couldn't put them into words.

This was the woman who'd carried his child. Their

child who had been Sam's only concern when she'd been delirious and out of her mind with fear and pain. How did he tell her what that did to him? Her bravery. Her sexy-as-hell grit.

The reality of how close he'd come to losing her, twice, shook through him.

Randy ran his hands up her quivering thighs. He couldn't take her with his body for fear of hurting her so soon after having the baby. But he could give her pleasure. He could block out everything for her but the reality that her body needed him.

When his mouth found her sweet center, she strained into his touch, accepting him. Struggling to get closer instead of pulling away.

SAM'S ARMS WERE FREE. She could have stopped Randy with just one touch. One word. She should stop them both from falling any deeper into this insanity.

Instead, she kissed him as if her life depended on it.

Her fingers curled into his hair. He was being gentle. Careful. She wanted the fire they'd shared. The need.

"Please," she begged. "Please take me away from here."

Randy's next kiss held the edge she craved.

"Where do you want to go?" He caressed her. Tantalized her.

Each stroke and kiss and touch took her higher. Made her want more, which he was eager to give. Seconds, minutes, an hour maybe. She had no idea how long the sweet torture lasted. Until one second her sanity was a questionable thing. Then the next, it was gone completely. She was free. Burning free as she shivered and strained, her body crying for more while she was held and loved and praised for every second of lost control.

"Again," Randy demanded. "Not enough. Let me feel it again."

Randy was already building her back up. Pulling the pieces of her together, only to begin scattering them again, with each stroke of his fingers and lips and voice.

Her hands tightened on his shoulders, trying to hold him back.

"Don't," she begged.

It was too good to be real, joining with someone this completely. And he still had most of his clothes on. She didn't want this. The responsibility of it. The perfection.

The next streak of pleasure called her a liar.

"I need…" she gasped. "I need…"

"Yes," Randy whispered. "I'm here."

"But you…" He was still separate, while she was falling apart beneath him.

He was an intense man. Aggressive in every part of his life. She could feel him holding back. Giving and taking nothing in return.

"You need—" she started to say.

"I need you." The gravelly sound of Randy's voice drove her excitement higher. "Just you."

The next wave crashed through her.

Her body wouldn't stop vibrating. Needing. Begging for more. She pulled until Randy was beside her, then beneath her as she crawled on top. She needed him naked beneath her. Now!

"No, baby." He grabbed for her hands. Stopped her from completely freeing him from his jeans. "You can't. We can't. It's too soon after the baby, and I won't be able to stop if you... Sam, don't," he wheezed as she bent to kiss her way down his chest.

The memory of holding him in her hands lured her. The sound of him needing her as much as she needed him. The promise of how good they could be together. The memory of it had her stroking him and telling him how much more she wanted.

"We can't," he grit out between clenched teeth.

She couldn't stop.

She couldn't let go.

"Please, let me—"

"Damn!" he gasped as she stroked him again. "You don't have to, Sam. You've already given me more than you know..."

Sam realized it wasn't wild sex she craved after all. The frenzy and blind escape of Savannah wasn't what she needed now. She needed to feel Randy lose himself for her. She needed the soul-deep connection he'd pushed them toward.

"Let me hear you come apart for me," she whispered.

Randy's mouth found hers. His kiss freed her to touch and stroke and entice him toward the same oblivion that he'd taken her.

Everything she couldn't say, she poured into her touch.

Oh, God.

I love him!

Sam kissed Randy back and clung to him. She abandoned herself to giving pleasure and feeling his unguarded response and holding every second of it as close as she could. And when Randy found his release, she let herself believe that the moment would never end. That they had forever to feel this perfect. This complete.

Shaking, still kissing her like he'd never stop, Randy turned her until he'd braced himself above her on shaking arms. He gazed down at her in a way that would shatter her if she didn't make it stop.

His arms snaked around her. "Are you okay?" he asked.

She was perfect. It had all been perfect. So perfect, she sat up. She scooted off the bed when he tried to reach for her again.

She grabbed the IV stand and shuffled to the spread that had been shoved to the bottom of the bed. She pulled it over her disheveled dress, too shaken to button herself back up yet.

She needed him. Randy's strength and passion and unshakable belief that they could carve something besides disaster out of all of this. She needed him beside her, protecting her and making her feel like they would have a lifetime of perfect moments like this.

She wanted it all.

But that didn't change the fact that Luca was just as determined to take it all away. And that meant Sam needed Randy out of it, now more than ever.

Not just because of the baby. It had never been just about the baby. She loved Randy. Maybe she'd loved him from their first night together. And she wouldn't watch another man she cared about be destroyed trying to save her.

It was time to let the dream go.

CHAPTER TWELVE

"NO," SAM SAID while Randy endured her pulling away from him. "I'm not okay. I wasn't okay the first time we met, and I'm not okay now. I'm being hunted. Someone wants me dead. No matter how amazing we are together in bed, that doesn't change reality."

Randy closed his eyes against her reasoning and the images that followed.

The darkness of the explosion at the last hotel. Their escape. Sam in labor, in pain, pinned in her crashed-up car...

He jerked his eyes back open, stunned by the riot of flashbacks. Once a crisis was over, he never remembered the scene. He debriefed with his team. He learned from every call. But he never held on to the emotion of the moment. It never got personal. Except there was nothing not personal about needing to protect Sam, or knowing that she was still determined to leave him. There was no way to block that kind of pain.

"Then I guess it's a good thing I'm not *with* you." He stood and pulled his clothes together, finding his T-shirt amidst their rumpled sheets.

As soon as he was off the bed, Sam sank back onto it, deflated. Alone already, though he was still in the room.

He even understood her survival instinct. The reflex not to connect. That's what made this harder. Because holding Sam had tempted him to believe that together they could beat their memories, as well as the man hunting her. For the first time in his life, Randy had let himself want a future with a woman. A woman who might always be running.

"I never expected any of this," he admitted. "I didn't expect to meet a stranger, and instantly feel more connected to her than I have anyone else in my life. But I did. I fought it, too. But that doesn't change what's happened. Or how unfair it is, expecting you to feel the same way in the midst of everything you're dealing with."

Sam inhaled slowly, as if steeling herself for an argument Randy wasn't up for.

He held up a hand.

"It's not your fault," he said. "You're not ready for something like this. I understand."

He didn't, but he had no business pushing any harder. Her life was impossible enough.

"I'll go see if I can get something more out of Dean," he said. "Take your time pulling yourself together."

Sam's silence followed him into the sitting area between the suite's two bedrooms. Determined to keep moving, Randy crossed to the other bedroom's door. He knocked but only waited a second before turning the knob and pushing his way inside. Pissed at the whole damn mess, he was ready to blast the first fed who crossed his path. But the people inside were already ripping each other to verbal shreds.

"I don't give a crap what kind of emotional state she's in," a female deputy said to Dean. "She deserves to know—"

"She knows what she has to know to keep her under control." The rigid set of Dean's jaw hinted that he hated what he was saying. The fist he'd clenched said he meant every word. "Otherwise, they're both dead. The baby's safe as long as her mother stays off Luca's radar. If Sam refuses to stay put, then—"

"What's happened to the baby?" Randy closed the door to the sitting room.

Sam might not see any place for him in her life, but she'd given him a precious gift that would always connect them. A daughter he planned to build his future around, even if Sam refused to be part of it.

Every eye in the room swiveled to Randy. No one responded.

"What don't you want Sam to know?" he demanded.

The new female agent took a controlled step back, as if she was bracing to counter an attack. Randy must have looked as deadly furious as he felt.

Good.

He pinned Dean with a *don't mess with me* scowl and finished tucking his shirt into his jeans. The hell with who wondered what about why his clothes were a mess.

"Your daughter's fine." Dean gave him his own bad-ass stare. "She's being treated in a regional care facility near where the rest of your family's been settled. One of your brothers and your sister are with her."

"*What* happened?" Randy bit out.

Logic. Facts. Realistic options. Those were what he needed to focus on. He'd been running on emotion for too long. Making decisions the way he had been got people killed when he was on the job. So far, they hadn't done a thing to help Sam or the baby, either.

It was time to stop feeling and start focusing.

Dean was staring at the floor. He looked up, inhaling. "On the drive to your family's new location, your daughter briefly stopped breathing."

Randy linked his hands behind his back and took his own deep breath.

God, Sam. When are you going to catch a break?

"She's…" He had to clear his voice before he could finish. "The baby, she's…"

"She's fine," Dean assured him.

"But…" *Facts. Focus on the facts, not on racing to your child or throttling Dean for considering keeping quiet about this.*

"There's a problem with her respiration," the female marshal said. "She—"

"Brown…" Dean warned.

"She's responding to treatment," Deputy Brown continued. "But there may be underlying causes that should be seen by a specialist. And—"

"Brown!" Dean stepped between Randy and the woman. "The marshals on the scene have the situation under control, and—"

"The marshals on the scene didn't have a preemie baby brother who died when he was ten days old because of an undiagnosed heart murmur!" Brown faced down her boss. "Their baby might be fine. She might not be. Either way, this is a decision for that child's parents to make. She needs to see a specialist."

"And she will," Dean agreed in a clipped voice. "Just not back in Atlanta. Not anywhere that someone might be looking for her."

"My daughter has a heart problem?" Randy managed to get out. "And you're discussing treatment options without consulting her mother or me?"

"There's no evidence—" Dean started to explain.

"You!" Randy grabbed the female agent's arm. "Brown, is it? Tell me what's happening with my child, if for no other reason than it will help me keep her mother from jumping out the nearest window and stealing a car to get to her."

Which Sam would do.

She might not know what the hell to do with her feelings for him. But Randy had no doubt she'd fight to the death to protect her sister and her daughter.

Brown hesitated.

"Someone has to trust me here." Randy switched his focus to Max Dean. "Sam doesn't. She doesn't trust any of you, either. But she'll listen to me. Tell me what I need to know about the baby, so I can help get through to her mother."

"What?" A gasp drew their attention toward the sitting room. No one had heard Sam open the door.

She was staring at Randy. "You're going to help them *get through to me?*"

"You don't understand." Crowding her was the wrong move, but Randy couldn't stop himself from stepping closer. "Just listen—"

"Oh, I understand fine." Sam backed away. "Sex didn't do the trick, so it's time to move on to using the baby? What? You're going to get whatever information you can from these guys, so you can use that to get to me!"

Randy rocked back on his heels. "I know you're afraid and you're convinced you're alone in all this. But I—"

"You'll do whatever it takes to get what you want. That's what you guys do."

"Us guys?"

Sam was terrified, but it wasn't of him. Randy was certain of that. She was still reeling from whatever was hounding her.

"You do whatever you have to, to get what you want." She pointed a finger at him. "You tell whatever lie works. Just like my protection detail. Nothing you say is the whole truth. Nothing you do is real. You're all just like Luca. Just like when he—"

"Sam, you need to calm down." Dean stepped to Randy's side.

"No," Randy insisted, "she needs to get this out, once and for all."

"The details about Luca are need-to-know," Dean argued. "And—"

"Oh, Randy knows plenty about the kind of man

Luca is," Sam insisted. "Don't you, Lieutenant Montgomery? You both know exactly how to make me believe. You make me care about you, and—"

"You care about me?" Randy repeated, holding his breath.

"Of course I do!" she shouted. "You make me feel safe. Just like him, you made me need you, no matter how dangerous it is. Satisfied? You win. Now it's time to turn it into something hateful and terrifying and destructive. Because I either have to let you go, or watch my brother come after you the way he did Peter!"

There wasn't a sound in the room.

"It's not going to turn into anything." Randy wouldn't let it. "I'm trying to make these bastards tell us what's going on with our daughter. Then we're going to figure this out together. Fight together. Because I… Wait. Your brother? Luca, the guy who killed your fiancé, is…your brother?"

"YES, LUCA GIANFRANCO is my brother," Sam said.

It was exactly the reality check they both needed to put an end to what they'd started in the other room.

"Let's take a break," Max said.

"Let's not." Sam waited for Randy to say something. Anything.

A stare was all she got. She'd been unkind and completely unfair. But at least the truth was out.

"I'm a threat to everyone I'm near." She realized he was standing too close again, and that she wanted him even closer. And that her growing dependence on Randy Montgomery terrified her far more than Luca Gianfranco ever had. "My entire family is."

"Revealing more about your past is a bad idea," Max cautioned.

"Putting this off so long was the bad idea, the hell with isolating my testimony until the grand jury hears it."

Sam was just as responsible as Luca for what had happened to her fiancé and her baby and the two deputies who'd died back at the hotel. She'd be responsible for anything that happened to Randy or his family. She'd been born into evil and had profited from it her entire childhood.

It didn't matter that she'd eventually tried to break free. She was a Gianfranco. Her family meant death to everyone who challenged her brother's control. She wouldn't let that happen to Randy, no matter how badly she needed him and their baby with her.

She stared up at him.

Their baby…

He and Max had been arguing when she came in, about—

"The baby? What were you saying about the baby? What's wrong?" She looked at the somber faces of the agents and saw the fear in Randy's eyes. "Tell me what's wrong with my daughter…"

The child who was God knew where, living with strangers, because Luca's homicidal insanity made it impossible for Sam to keep her.

The agents filtered out, leaving Sam to stare at

Max. A hand soothed down her hair, over and over. It was a calming touch. Randy's touch.

She jerked away.

Randy didn't move from her side. His expression grew murderous as he looked at Max.

"Tell us what's happening with our daughter," he insisted. "Enough with the half truths you think will keep Sam safe, or keep her testimony secure. Tell us the goddamn truth, and what your people plan to do about it!"

Max's arms were crossed. His game face was on. Then he nodded.

"Your daughter is stable," he said. "But on the trip to her new location she momentarily stopped breathing. It may—"

"What!" Sam wilted onto one of the beds. She clenched her fingers so tightly she couldn't feel them. Only it was Randy's hand she had in a death grip. He was sitting beside her.

"The doctors are saying it may be only a minor respiratory problem," Max added. "It could have been due to the way she'd been positioned in her car seat. She's been checked out by doctors at a trauma center near her new location, and they haven't found any other physical symptoms. They're keeping her overnight, but—"

"At a regional hospital?" Sam asked. "What if they don't have the equipment to diagnose the problem? What if—"

"She's being closely observed," Max assured her. "They have what they'll need to help her. If there are any new breathing issues, they'll—"

"How far are they from Atlanta? There have to be specialists who can—"

"You mean Atlanta doctors who specialize in dealing with complications that arise with newborns?" Max asked. "The kind of doctors your brother would be having watched, now that he knows you gave birth in Atlanta? The bomb at the hotel means Luca's on your trail again. Which means I have a leak of some kind on my hands, and—"

"But if she's sick—"

"Your daughter's with the Montgomerys. She's fine."

"But—"

Randy squeezed her hand to stop her.

"What about what that deputy said?" he asked. "Why was Brown talking about heart problems? What aren't you telling us?"

Max shoved his hands into his pockets instead of responding.

"She's my daughter," Sam pleaded. A little girl Sam hadn't let herself name for fear she'd grow too attached. Now, she might be dying. "My daughter's sick and I can't even hold her. I may never…see her again, if my brother has his way. The least you can do is be honest with us about what's happening to her."

Us…

The word felt so right with Randy there beside her.

"The doctor said respiratory problems in a child so young could be a symptom of a congenital heart defect," Max finally admitted. "They're monitoring the baby through the night. In the morning they'll decide if she needs to be seen by someone at a children's hospital."

Randy's head dropped. "But you think taking her to a larger hospital would almost guarantee putting her on Gianfranco's radar."

"A newborn popping up with a need for specialized care?" Max asked. "No matter what precautions we took, we'd risk another leak. Gianfranco's too well connected. The grand jury's set to call for Sam's testimony. Luca will be more motivated than ever to silence her."

"But you'll protect the baby." Sam clung to Randy's arm to pull herself to her feet. "You promised you'd protect her and Gabby."

"Yes." Max had never sounded more determined. "We'll protect all of you as best we can, given the circumstances we're dealing with."

"Circumstances I'm responsible for." Sam swallowed, nausea creeping up the back of her throat.

"This isn't your fault," Randy insisted, standing with her. "You—"

"I'm the one who tried to leave my family's world and have a normal life. I'm the one who got my fiancé shot. I'm the one who ran without thinking what that would mean for my baby sister, then ran again from the people trying to keep us safe. Exactly whose fault do you think it is?"

"You're just scared and off-balance, Sam."

"And look what I've let that fear do! All this time, I thought I was fighting back. I was going to stop Luca for good. Now we can't even get our daughter the medical care she needs. Luca wants me, not her. Maybe I should just go back to New York. That way you could—"

"No!" Randy said. "Going back to that bastard is out of the question."

"That bastard is my brother. He'll kill you to get to me. *That's* who I am. There's no stopping what my family is, no matter what I say in court. No matter how hard I fight it. All of this… What you're trying to do, what you're wanting me to become…" What she wanted now, too. "It's pointless, and the sooner I accept that, the safer everyone will be. I—"

Randy's kiss begged her to stop.

"You're not like your brother," he insisted.

"I'm part of his world." She'd give anything to be free of the darkness. For her daughter. For Randy and his family. For herself. "And my testimony won't be enough to protect any of us, will it?" she asked Max. "My brother is too powerful. Too connected."

"Testifying is a start, Sam," Max said. "You have to see the big—"

"A start?" Randy asked. "If this doesn't end with her testimony, then when?"

When Max said nothing, Randy's attention shifted back to her. This was the real nightmare. Having him there, wanting their daughter, wanting her. And Sam maybe even believing him a little when he said he'd stay, no matter what.

It was a dream wrapped in a nightmare.

"This doesn't end until Luca ends it," she finally accepted, an idea blooming along with the need to rip her dream away from her brother's control. "Which means my only chance to really be free of it, is to draw my brother out. He has to be the one to do something stupid for a change. Meanwhile, he'll be so distracted, the Montgomerys will be able to get our daughter the specialized help she needs. I have to—"

"Sam," Max cautioned. "We're going to stick to the plan, until—"

"No," Sam said over him. "What if…"

The idea was still half formed, but it was there. It had always been there, but she'd been too afraid to face what she had to do. Then Randy had come back to her. And thanks to him and their baby, Sam could finally see what had to be done.

"What if we use me as bait," she said, "so this can finally end, once and for all?"

CHAPTER THIRTEEN

SAM GLARED at Max while she ignored Randy.

"You know I'm right," she said to her federal agent. "It's the only way we all get what we want out of this. You get Luca's head on a platter. The people I care about are safe."

"By doing what?" Randy demanded.

"By giving my brother a target he can go after— me, because I'm racing to save my newborn and being careless, the way I've been careless every step of the way up till now."

"You want to use our child as bait?"

"No, just me. The baby will stay safe with your family. All I need is for Luca to believe—"

"—that you're taking our child to see a specialist?" Randy sounded sick. "It'll be too easy a mark for him to pass up, right? He won't be able to resist, and when the feds catch his men trying to kill you, again, they'll have even more ammunition against the bastard."

Max glanced at the arm Randy had circled around Sam's waist. He glanced at the BlackBerry he held in his hand. The device never stopped chirping for his attention. He finally looked at Sam.

"The federal prosecutor would very much like to have more to throw at Luca," he said. "My information says your brother may even be on the field of play himself now. Personally engaged in your pursuit for the first time, because—"

"Because his minions keep botching things when they try to kill her!" Randy pulled Sam to his side. "Now he's hitting the A-T-L to personally kick ass and take names, so things are looking up?"

"If Sam wants a guarantee you can all have your lives back—" Max shrugged "—this might be your best shot."

"You said the grand jury's about to call her testimony."

"Which is why Luca's so revved up." Sam reveled in the feel of Randy still holding her close, still wanting her, no matter what she'd said and done.

Just give me this chance to make it right.

She finally felt like she had a chance. Luca coming to Atlanta was a mistake. It was reckless. Her normally unemotional brother didn't trust anyone else to finish Sam off.

"You couldn't have planned this any better if you'd tried." Randy turned on Max.

"This was my idea," Sam said.

"This ridiculous plan, yes. But what about that call you made to your sister that started this?" he demanded. "That's how your brother's men found you when your protection wasn't around. Pretty damn convenient. How close were you going to let Luca get back at the hotel?" Randy asked Max. "I'm assuming the explosives and losing two deputies wasn't in the prosecution's plan to catch themselves a mobster, but you never know. Drawing this maniac out once the legal pressure was on—that's been the goal from the start, right?"

Max measured the way Randy was balanced on the balls of his feet, his muscled chest straining against his T-shirt. Max calmly pocketed his Black-Berry. He took off his jacket, folded it with careful deliberation and placed it over the edge of the bed. When he crossed his arms, his own muscles threatened to bust the seams of his starched dress shirt.

Sam laid a palm on Randy's shoulder, holding him back. Still, parts of what he'd said rang true. Not that it mattered—she was determined to end things with her brother before anyone else got hurt. But had she really let herself be played that easily?

"Is it true?" she asked Max.

"It might be advisable," her marshal said to Randy instead of her, "not to throw around accusations when you don't know the first damn thing about this situation beyond how quickly you want to get in Sam's pants every time you two are alone together."

Randy tensed to launch himself at Max. Sam grabbed him with both hands, aggravating her shoulder. She tried to hold the pain in, but a gasp escaped. Randy turned to her, relaxing so that she could let go without worrying about him attacking a federal marshal.

He pulled her close, fitting her head beneath his chin and softly rubbing her shoulder.

"You're a manipulative bastard," he said to Max. "That's what I know. And things got considerably more promising for you and your team and this prosecutor you're fronting for, once this pretend life you've shoved Sam into went to shit. Now you've got her offering herself up for even more danger. If you didn't plan it, I find it hard to believe you didn't at least give her enough space to be reckless enough to expose herself to Gianfranco's people."

"Sam—" Max started to say.

"Don't *Sam* me in that *you're my big brother* voice." She was holding back tears, and she hated it. She was sick and tired of feeling weak and helpless. "My real big brother's a psychopath. The role doesn't come highly recommended. Tell me Randy's just being paranoid. Tell me that you had no idea I'd run to Savannah, until I got back and you read me the riot act. Tell me you didn't know I'd called my sister and alerted Luca that you'd hidden me in Macon, until I turned up banged up on an Atlanta interstate. Tell me…"

One more lie she'd believe…

She turned her face into Randy's strong chest.

"I didn't know, either time," Max insisted. "But…"

"But?" Randy asked for her. "Don't stop now, Marshal Dean. Tell us exactly how your team's managed to mess Sam's protection up so completely—on purpose."

"But," Max continued. "I've been recently informed that you've had a shadow, since the first day we placed you."

"A shadow?" she forced out.

"An agent *not* on the U.S. Marshals Service's payroll has been watching you. Protectees are relocated and ones as high profile as Sam are carefully monitored with regular check-ins. But my team wasn't approved for continuous observation until after your accident."

"So who approved Sam being tailed?" Randy asked.

"The federal prosecutor," Sam offered. "Or someone he works for who thought I just might be enough of a wild card to draw my brother out. Looks like they were right. All they had to do was postpone my hearing before the grand jury long enough for me to come completely unglued."

Max hesitated.

Then he nodded.

"I was only made aware of it today," he said, "when we arrived here. I was debriefed while you two were…cleaning up. There are logs of every move you've made since coming under our protection, and corresponding records of when your brother's operation picked up your trail in Macon—using a tap on your sister's phone. I was only notified of a possible breach after enough time had passed to lure your brother's men closer in. By then, you'd already run, Sam. I'm not sure how they tagged your car so quickly, but—"

"My brother has eyes everywhere. Less than half an hour after I called Gabriella, there was a car I'd never seen before parked across the street. It followed me to the grocery store. It followed me back home. Not too close. Never completely out of sight. So I…

I ran. Again. While the federal prosecutor who was supposed to be protecting me waited to see what would happen. Just like when I ran from Luca in New York."

Just like when Luca had killed…

"Peter?" She felt behind her for the bed as her legs gave out again. "Were they…was someone watching me back then? When Luca… Were they there when I ran from my fiancé's bed?" She glared at Max. "You bastards were there, even then, weren't you?"

"It wasn't the Marshals Service," Max started to explain. "We wouldn't have—"

"Of course you would! Someone watched while I ran and talked myself into asking for help. Then the prosecutor swooped in to save me. But he didn't bother to stop Luca before he killed Peter, did he? Not when he could build a better case once I was alone and willing to do anything to get Gabby out." Sam found herself in Max's face. "All this time, I thought I was fighting to be free, and you people were just playing me to get what you wanted."

Randy pulled Sam away and settled her back to the bed. He knelt in front of her. He brushed back the hair that her tears had matted against her face.

"You're not alone," he said. "Never again. I'm here."

And he wanted to always be there. But that couldn't happen. Not while Sam's brother was hunting her.

"Another agency was monitoring you in New York," Max admitted. "Their parameters at the time were only to follow you when you left your home. No one knew Peter Grant was dead until after you'd run, and by then Luca had covered his tracks. The only way to prosecute him was to convince you to testify to witnessing the murder. My agency came on board then. Hiding you until your testimony became my job. You were green-lighted for federal relocation. I had no idea other agents would continue monitoring your movements and your communications. Or that years of delay would keep you and your sister from moving on with your lives. You have to believe me, Sam."

"Actually," Randy stood with an ease that mocked the nausea and weakness creeping through Sam. "She doesn't. She doesn't have to do anything with you people anymore. No more blindly following your bogus *protection* guidelines while the government uses her as bait. No more guarantee that she's going to testify for the prosecutor. No more believing you have her and her sister and now her baby's best interests in mind. No more believing anything you people try to pass off for the truth. She—"

"How soon?" Sam asked.

"What?" both men said.

"How soon do you want to take me back to Atlanta Memorial?" she asked Max. "I'm assuming that's the easiest place for me to pop up on Luca's radar. How quickly can you pull a plan together?"

"You're going to let these people throw you at your brother again?" Randy was staring at the floor instead of looking at her.

Keep believing in me, she silently begged him. *Please give me a chance to make this right.*

"I'm done pretending that anything else will work but facing my brother," she said out loud.

Randy had every right to walk away from her. From all of this. But she knew now that she'd never stop needing him. Wanting him. Loving him.

If there was even the slightest chance she could have that kind of love in her life, to have Randy and their daughter with her for real...

It was a dream Sam was going to fight for.

She looked around Randy to Max.

"Tell me how and when this can happen. And don't even think about bullshitting me. I'll do whatever you need me to do to draw Luca out. But you take care of him for good this time. And once Luca's focused on me, you get my daughter to a specialist. Tell me how you're going to protect the Montgomerys and Gabby and the baby and Randy. Tell me how you're going to get them all someplace safe while we do this, and you better make it damn convincing. Because if I'm not satisfied with your plan, I don't move from this spot. And the federal prosecutor can forget about my testimony. We either do this right this time, or I'm done for good."

HER BROTHER.

Luca Gianfranco was Sam's brother, and she was determined to take him on.

Randy closed his eyes as he listened to Max Dean work the angles with his team. Randy and Sam were sitting on opposite sides of the suite's den. She hadn't looked at him since giving Dean her ultimatum—since she'd lumped Randy in with everyone else she expected the feds to protect while she went on the offensive against the mob.

She was digging deep for the courage to make her stand. To fight back. Maybe even to fight for them. But she still wanted Randy out of it. She was convinced she had to do this alone. That he couldn't possibly understand what she was facing or know what he was getting into by confronting the danger with her.

He approached her, hurting for both of them. He hadn't been here in a long time, desperately needing someone and not knowing if he could have her. Not since he'd watched the police drag his mother to jail, then the court officers take her to prison. He didn't know how to handle the doubt and fear raging through him, any better than he had when he'd been a child. All he knew was that shutting the feelings away, keeping things in-control, wasn't going to reach Sam. And if he didn't reach her now, he was going to lose her for good. That he was certain of.

She was sitting on one of the den's couches, her legs drawn to her chest, her good arm hugging her knees close. When he sat beside her, she let her body fall toward him. As if it was the most natural thing in the world for her to want to be held by him.

"How dangerous is your brother?" He kept his voice pitched low, while Max and his team continued to strategize.

Sam looked up, fear clouding her bright eyes. She reached for his hand.

"Luca told me to stop dating Peter," she said. "Not because Peter was a threat to the business, or even because Luca didn't think he was good enough for me. It was a test. My brother has to know that everyone around him is one hundred percent loyal. It's the way his world functions."

"A test?" Randy rubbed his thumb over the satin of her palm.

"Would I give up what I wanted most for my brother? For the family? Would I give Luca my dreams, if he asked me to?"

"And you wouldn't."

Just like she was refusing to now.

"I was so young." Sam smiled, as if she pitied the woman she'd been. "It was only two years ago, but it feels like a lifetime. I didn't realize what I was risking when I went to Peter's that night. I swear. I just knew I wanted out for good. And I believed Peter could protect me."

"And your brother—"

"Luca was going to have my undivided devotion. Otherwise, I was nothing to him. My life, Gabby's life. They're just pawns in this game my brother's been playing since my father died. And…"

"And after your brother destroyed your life, you decided you'd never let anyone close enough to hurt you like that again."

Just like Randy had learned to push everyone away. He'd reunited with his siblings. He'd let them in enough to relearn how to trust them. But trusting his heart to someone—he hadn't believed that depth of love was possible for him. Until now. But could the woman he was falling for believe along with him?

"Tell me you're going to let me in, Sam. Let me fight through this with you and be there when it's over. Tell me you can believe in us enough not to give up now."

CHAPTER FOURTEEN

"THERE HAVE BEEN CALLS?" Luca Gianfranco asked the man who was standing in front of his desk trying not to look terrified. "How many? About what, specifically?"

"Several within the last few hours—to the hospital's top neonatologist. One of the nurses on the floor has been brought in to consult. And the chief of staff. All about a case no one will confirm exists. Our sources there say security's on overdrive, but there's no apparent reason. Something big is rumored to be happening tomorrow morning."

Luca sat still as stone in his leather chair. The lights of the Atlanta skyline rose in stately grandeur outside his office's windows. Atlanta was one of half a dozen cities that his organization operated from. It was key to have a strong presence in top U.S. locations, as well as several in Europe, Asia, Canada and South America.

And thanks to his southeastern contacts, intel was pouring in hourly. He had no doubt that he'd have what he needed to shore up the holes Sam had punched in his reputation. But the man cowering in front of Luca had damn well better be doubting whether Luca would allow him to continue breathing.

"Tomorrow morning?" Luca asked him. "Given everything our sources have been able to dig up, you're sure that's the time to strike?"

"Yes," replied one of Luca's childhood playmates. "I'm certain of it."

"You were certain when you located Sam in Macon and pursued her without authorization. You were certain she was taken care of when you instigated her accident. Then you informed me that she'd died at the hospital, only she turned up alive, back in protection with a baby in tow. You pinpointed her next location and were certain that you and your men could take care of Sam and her handlers before I could arrive on the scene and give my own orders. You want me to believe you didn't even know she was pregnant in the first place. Tell me why I should stake my organization's future on the information you're bringing me now?"

Carlos Forrelli had the good sense to pause before answering. He was a smart man. Smarter than Luca, as a matter of fact. But wisdom wasn't the same thing, and the Forrellis had always been on the losing end of that spectrum.

"Certain enough to stake your life on it?" Luca wondered out loud. "Because that's what you're asking me to do. To trust your loyalty and commitment to me, enough to act on this latest information. And you're standing there looking less than certain now. As if you don't want to be here, facing me after all the problems you've caused. Maybe this is another mistake?"

"I've confirmed with three different sources. Inside the hospital, the APD and our man in the marshals service." Carlos squared his shoulders and morphed back into the confident, dangerous man Luca had once respected. "These are people who have our organization to thank for their homes and their children's private schools. We've paid their debts, paid for their rehab, and paid for their habits when they fell off the wagon. We know every detail of their lives. Their loyalty to us is unquestionable. Your sister and her sick newborn are due back at Atlanta Memorial tomorrow morning."

"And these same loyal, dependent sources will be able to provide me with logistics about the best way to introduce myself to my niece? That little girl belongs with her family. Her mother has to be stopped once and for all."

"You'll have all the information you need. We're receiving hourly text messages. Our men are analyzing all possible entries and exits from the hospital complex. Wherever they take Sam, we'll get to her. I'd stake my own son's life on it."

"You're that certain." Luca smiled reassuringly. "I want to give you this last chance to make things up to me, Carlos. Your wife and your son—they're precious parts of my family. I wanted to give *them* this one final opportunity to be proud of you. We all want you to succeed. Is that what's going to happen this time?"

"You have my word," Carlos promised. "Come tomorrow morning, nothing will stand in your way."

"Excellent work. Well done." Luca lifted his father's automatic from where he'd held it hidden in his lap and fired three quick rounds—two into Carlos's chest, the final one a head shot. As the stunned man dropped, Luca added, "Rest assured that you have *my* word. Your family will be under my protection for the rest of their lives."

"I'M GOING TO BE at Atlanta Memorial in the morning," Charlie repeated. "Any feds standing in my way are going to get knocked on their asses on my way out of the door."

It was a good line. Too bad the petite woman challenging his decision was a whole lot scarier when she was mad than any federal marshal. And Emma was spitting mad.

"Randy's off playing hero with a woman he barely knows, while some maniac's trying to kill her. Now you're dead set on chasing danger back to Atlanta, too, thinking you being there is going to somehow make things better. Get over yourself, little brother."

It was true. Charlie likely couldn't do anything more than the professionals executing the deadly bait and switch at Atlanta Memorial. But—

"I have to be there." He couldn't shake the feeling. "I promised Randy I'd have his back. You and the baby are safe here. And… I have to be there."

Emma sighed, the fight going out of her. She gave Charlie her non-smile and patted him on the shoulder on her way to the tiny hospital bed. Their niece was sleeping. Breathing better. But still not out of the woods.

Emma had raised three teenage boys and a daughter of her own. She knew better than to hug and cling and beg one of them to be reasonable, once their minds were set. Top that with her being the toughest public defender in town, and she understood Charlie and his brothers' compulsion to follow their instincts and put everything on the line.

"Glinda said Randy wouldn't be going with Sam," Emma reasoned. She pulled the baby's blanket higher to combat the hotel's prevailing chill. "He's supposed to be transported here, to be with us once Sam's en route."

Charlie stared down at a soft, fuzzy duck he was holding. One of the baby's rattles. He was the oldest brother, only five years younger than Emma. He'd been eleven when their lives had been blown to hell. Surviving Family Services had ripped away what was left of Charlie's childhood. The trauma of all of it had obliterated his memories from before that.

All he'd known once they had become a family again, was that his life was going to be about preventing the kind of emptiness that still lurked inside him from happening to other kids. Other families. He and his brothers had all become firefighters to save strangers. But also to save themselves. To be there in a crisis and to fight, where they'd once felt powerless. To protect and to remind themselves daily that they could control the uncontrollable, no matter how improbable the circumstances.

"I don't care what's happened between Randy and Sam in the last twelve hours, or what Glinda said about her team's plans." Charlie loosened his death grip on the rattle. "Do you really think for a moment that Randy's going to walk away from Sam? The woman he's dragged away from two disasters now, after not being able to get her off his mind since their one-night stand?"

Emma stared at Charlie from across the tiny hotel room. "Probably not."

"No way is Randy coming here," Charlie insisted, "while Sam faces this Luca character."

And no way was Charlie going to sit on his hands and wait to hear whether his brother had gotten himself killed. Randy had a chance now. A chance to hold on to a family of his own that he deserved. He couldn't lose that. Charlie had to make sure of it.

"They're not going to let you out of here," Emma said. "No way are they going to let a fireman barge in on their operation back in town."

"Who's waiting for an invitation?"

Charlie had a brother-in-law back at the hotel, grilling the federal marshals about tomorrow's plans. He had the rest of his family to run interference, including his larger-than-life brother and adorably sneaky niece, both of whom could distract a saint into accidentally giving Satan a hall pass to heaven. What better cover could a guy ask for?

"I'm going," he said. "And I need help, Em. I need you with me on this one."

He could sense his sister's fear. He could see the

traces of panic crowding her normally unflappable optimism. Then, just as quickly, the hands she'd been wringing snapped to her hips. She shook her head at him, and there was a flash of pride in the smile that followed.

"You boys are trying to do me in," she said.

It had been her chief complaint all those years, her only complaint. And every time she said it, each of them had known what she meant was, *I love you. I'll do anything for you. Anything...*

"I'm assuming you're going to want Rick's help giving our security the slip?" she surmised. "Maybe Martin Rhodes or some of his buddies could be waiting at a side entrance to the hospital, to get you into town quickly?"

Kate's husband, Martin, was on permanent disability from the APD, but he was a big dog at the police academy. What they were about to ask him to do would cost him dearly. But Charlie had no doubt the guy would be there. That's what families did. And it had never been clearer just how large the Montgomerys' extended Atlanta family had become.

"Whatever it takes," Charlie said. "Randy's not going to be thinking clearly. I need to be there tomorrow. I'll know what he's going through. I'll know how he'll react. If you can get me the information about whatever the feds have planned and then get me to Atlanta, I'll take care of him, Emma. I promise."

Emma left their sleeping niece and walked into Charlie's open arms.

"You better take care of you both," Emma said against his shoulder. "You boys. You're trying to do me in...."

CHAPTER FIFTEEN

TELL ME YOU BELIEVE in us enough not to give up now.

Instead of answering, Sam had sat there with her heart in her eyes, fear consuming her features, while Randy fought the urge to demand that she stop doubting herself and him and what they could have together.

Then Max Dean had launched into his team's plans for tomorrow's sting—none of which factored Randy into Sam's suicidal trip back to Atlanta Memorial. Once the marshal had finished, Sam had walked into her and Randy's bedroom like a zombie.

Randy should let her go.

But there he was, standing in the bedroom doorway.

"You're hiding from me again," he said.

Sam was sitting on the edge of the bed. The sheets and bedspread they'd shoved aside earlier were scattered around her. She didn't look up.

"I believe in you, Randy…" Her voice caught on his name. "I believe you're the best thing that's ever happened to me. And you'll be the best father I could have asked for, for our daughter. You're the most amazing man I've ever met."

"But not amazing enough to include *us* in your

plans with the feds who've been playing you for two years? Tell me why you have to do this alone. Tell me how to make you believe that my place is with you, fighting with you, whatever happens next."

She shot him a stare of disbelief.

"Don't you think I want you there tomorrow? I've always wanted you…." She looked terrified by what she'd said. "Why would you keep putting your life on the line like that? Max still isn't sure who his leaks are. This is a disaster waiting to happen."

"Because—" Randy sat beside her and turned her shoulders until she was facing him "—if it wasn't for you, I'd never have known what this feels like. After the destruction that my parents' marriage was for my sister and brothers and me, this shouldn't be possible, needing you this way. Now *just getting by* isn't enough." His eyes pleaded with her. "Don't shut me out, Sam."

"Your parents? Randy, I'm not talking about domestic squabbles and an unhappy childhood. My brother's business destroys people's lives. He's destroyed mine. When someone stands in his way, they die!"

Randy felt his hold on his past slipping, because his memories weren't his to keep anymore. Not while he asked Sam to trust him with the scariest parts of her.

"I stood between my father and my mother," he forced himself to say, "while my old man tried to kill her. I dared him to come after me instead of my mother or Emma or one of my brothers, even though I was the smallest of the bunch. And I was standing there the night my mother grabbed his gun and shot him in the head to protect us."

Randy closed his eyes against the flashbacks, and the rush of guilt that came with not being able to stop what had happened. The same guilt that he knew was convincing Sam to fight alone now.

Then her touch was there, against his cheek, pulling him away from the emptiness. Her fingers were cool. Clean. The compassion she was offering promised forever as her fingers soothed away his frown.

"I know what evil is Sam." He pressed his forehead against hers. "I've spent a lifetime trying to fix that one night. My mother went to prison for protecting me. She died there. Now I give other people the second chance my mother gave my brothers and sister and me. But it's never been enough. It's never been real. Until now. Until I found you, feeling has meant living that moment over and over again and never getting to the other side of it."

Sam kissed him. She was crying. For him. And she was clinging to him as desperately as he was holding on to her.

"I'm so sorry," she said. And she was. She was right there with him, understanding the way no one else could. "You were just a little boy."

"I don't remember ever feeling like a little boy. I just remember being terrified, and deciding that I never wanted to feel that way again."

Sam nodded.

"What was her name?" she asked. "What was your mother's name?"

Randy breathed in. Hard. The air wouldn't release until he stopped trying to hold back the pain that came with his mother's memory.

"Jasmine." He hadn't said her name since her funeral. "My mother's name was Jasmine. She was the most beautiful woman I've ever known, until I met you." He drank in the acceptance shining from Sam's gaze. "She gave up everything to save us."

"And look how proud you've made her." Sam smiled. "Look at how you've survived. I think Jasmine would be very proud of the life you've created."

"Would she? Am I alive? Are you?" He watched Sam's smile fade and hated causing her more pain. But this moment was too important for both of them. "Surviving isn't enough, Sam. I want to live—with you. Because I… I love you. And I love our daughter. I'm not sure what that word means. I've never said it to anyone. But there'll never be anyone else I'll want to say it to. You're the one. Help me figure all this out. Help me build a life. Let me help *you*."

"You…" Sam's forehead wrinkled in confusion. A lone tear rolled down her cheek. "You love a mob princess who—"

"Who didn't ask to be born into any of this." Randy caught the flicker of doubt in her gaze. "What matters to me is now. And for the first time, I care about what happens tomorrow and the next day."

"I…" Sam kissed him. She buried her head against his neck. "Do you really believe there's a next day for people like us?"

"I believe in you," Randy whispered, his mouth near

her ear, "and what you mean to me. To our daughter. I believe you're something amazing that I can build my life around. Can you believe in that, too?"

"I…" Sam shook her head. "I can't even think of a baby name. What kind of mother does that make me?"

"You'll name her," he promised, "once you and Gabby are safe. Once you accept that you don't have to do this alone. Any of it. Whatever happens, you can trust me to be there, no matter what."

"Not tomorrow." Sam made a halfhearted move to pull away, but she let him catch her close again. "You can't be with me while I do this."

"I can't be anywhere else." Randy pulled her into his lap, refusing to let go. "You're the future I could never see. A future that's worth fighting for."

RANDY, talking about the future. *Their* future.

Sam had never wanted to believe in anything more.

"Peter offered me a future, and he died for it." It was the one truth Randy's logic couldn't reason away. "Our daughter needs—"

"She needs both her parents," Randy argued. "We'll give her that."

"You don't know what you're saying." Sam and Gabby—there was no guarantee where they'd be relocated. "You can't—"

"No, I can't," Randy agreed. "Not by myself. But *we* can do anything. I'm not stupid, Sam. I'm scared shitless. But I'm done running from what I'm feeling. Are you?"

Sam swallowed.

Then she was nodding. Clinging. Showing Randy that she wanted to believe, too, even if she still couldn't put what her heart was feeling into words.

"And tonight?" she asked. "Tonight can be just about—"

"—now," he finished for her.

It was the promise they'd made each other in Savannah.

She grazed his jaw with her lips. His chin. She shivered as his hands stroked up her back. Her own fingers dug into his muscled strength.

"Just now," he promised.

Her mind traveled back to the abandon, the freedom, the perfection of what they'd found at that shadowy, Low Country hotel. It hadn't felt empty, even then, when she'd reached for a stranger to get her through a desperate night. He'd become a lifeline she could hold on to. A hero she'd secretly wanted to keep forever.

"Randy…" His lips opened at the very first brush of hers. "You make me want to…"

He eased her back to the bed, as if she were the most precious thing in his world.

"Believe…" The word was filled with need, promising her every impossible thing she'd been running from. "You can do that, Sam. I know you can."

"Love me." She pulled his shirt free, baring his hard chest for the scrape of his nails.

"But you're…" He was trying to slow her down, to ease back.

"Be with me again." She pulled him closer. "Help

me… I need to know this is real. All of you. I need all of you again."

He stilled her hands where they were fumbling with his jeans. He smiled at her pout of frustration. His teeth nipped her bottom lip, then he made quick work of his belt and the rest. He dealt with the endless buttons down her dress.

His palms curved around her breasts. Her breath rushed out with his. Her next inhale was a needy, begging sound as his fingers explored and zeroed in on where she was most sensitive. His smile made her entire body throb. The knowing gleam in his eyes, the honesty shining there, sent Sam flying, free, opening her up. Her heart and her mind and her soul.

"Love," she whispered when they were skin to skin and he'd settled against the center of her. He was hard and as desperate as she was. "Love me, Randy. Always. No matter what…"

"No matter what," he promised.

Their joining was the gentlest, most erotic moment of her life. Randy's need was a fire burning through his touch, then through her blood until she was dizzy with it. But his body was careful, easy, while he watched her. Cherished her. Protected her.

"You can't hurt me." Her body cradled him closer, arching and begging for more. "Not unless you stop."

"Not a chance, baby."

His hands, his body, his gaze stroked her. His talented fingers slid low to torture her with even more pleasure. From that first touch eight months ago, he'd known exactly how to make her come apart.

"We could be really good together," he promised as she watched his control shatter, too. "Stop running, Sam, and believe…."

CHAPTER SIXTEEN

"YOU TWO ARE window dressing," Max said from the front passenger seat of the SUV. "That's understood before we move an inch from this spot. We insert you safely, then you both stay put until this is done."

Sam stared out the window at the lodge. She was ready for what had to happen with Luca. But letting last night go was a different thing. Last night had been a perfect, timeless place neither she nor Randy should have been able to believe in. But somehow, together, they had.

With morning had come the feeling that time was running out again.

"We show up at Atlanta Memorial and look suitably concerned," she parroted back. "Got it."

They'd gone over and over the plan, after Max had stopped fuming about Randy's insistence on coming along. Max was nervous, or he never would have lost his cool. And her federal marshal was never, ever nervous. Not a reassuring development while Sam struggled to believe that having Randy face Luca with her was the right decision—the only decision for both of them.

"We wait like live bait in the well-protected, private office of the half-finished physicians' center attached to the hospital," she continued. "You'll have cleared the entire place, except for your people. A doctor and a nurse will get us settled and take our daughter's stand-in away, then Luca shows up to finish me off."

"He'll never get near you," Max assured her. "APD and FBI will be swarming the place, all plain clothes. The site will be secure, agents and deputies only."

"But?" Randy asked, speaking up for the first time. He'd let Sam take the lead soothing Max. "If you're so confident Luca will know we're coming, there's a good chance your leak will be on site as well, right?"

"After the debacle at the first hotel, yes," Max admitted. "It's very likely."

"So why wouldn't he know this office you're taking us to will be flooded with feds and local law enforcement?"

"We suspect he will."

Sam's empty stomach cramped.

"But…" Randy squeezed her fingers.

"But we have contingency plans in place," Max half explained, "to deal with that possibility."

"So much for window dressing." Sam reminded herself that she'd agreed to this. That Randy had volunteered to put himself between her and Luca.

Because he loved her, not just because of the baby or because he felt responsible. And Randy was fighting for her to believe in the same future he saw, when all she could really see at the moment was Peter's stunned expression after Luca shot him.

"Maybe we shouldn't—" she started to say.

"Hold on." Max's hand went to the device attached to his ear. He turned forward while he listened. "Repeat that," he said. Several seconds passed. "You're sure…"

Randy's thumb stroked Sam's hand.

His gaze never left her.

"I'm scared," she admitted.

"Me, too," he said simply. "But we'll make this work."

"Where was he…" Max nodded at whatever answer he received. He glanced into the backseat. "At least we know the target's in the area. He's rattled enough to be careless, or he's sending a message. Either way, we've got the situation we wanted. We're on the road."

Sam held tighter to Randy, fear settling deep.

How much did her brother know? How much was Luca willing to risk to get to her?

"Your brother's in Atlanta," Max said. "And he just might be desperate enough to take our bait."

"And you know this how?" Randy asked.

"We have no flight records of him landing at any area airports. But…"

"Just say it!" Sam yanked her hand from Randy.

Max hesitated.

"APD found a body near your brother's Atlanta office this morning," he said. "Shot through the head."

"One of Luca's men?" Randy asked.

Sam's ears were ringing too loudly to manage the question on her own. How could she be walking back into her nightmare and dragging the man she loved with her?

"One of his point men for southeastern operations," Max said. "We—"

"Which one?" Sam had to know. "Which of his lieutenants did he execute?"

Max hesitated.

"Which one of his men did my brother kill, to send a message to me and anyone who might get in his way today?"

"Carlos Forrelli."

Sam slumped deeper into her seat. "Carlos is…was my cousin." Family. Nothing was sacred to Luca anymore. "Our aunt Tina's youngest. Just a year older than me. We grew up together in New York. Went to school together. Played together every afternoon. Carlos would walk me home from school, no matter what else he had going on. That made him my father's favorite. Then Luca's. They knew I'd be safe with him. My father promised my aunt that Carlos would always have a place in the family. How could my father not take care of someone who was that committed to taking care of me? He… I… one night, I even told Luca I might be in love with him. It was just a silly crush but…"

That had been fifteen years ago. It seemed like just yesterday. She and Luca and Carlos had been inseparable. Now, look what had happened.

"He was one of the men who've been after Sam?" Randy asked.

"Him or one of his people," Max said. "He's been doing a lousy job of getting her back to Luca, to the point that we've thought maybe he was intentionally letting her slip out of his grasp."

"On purpose?" Sam asked.

Had Carlos been why she and the baby had survived the accident? Why whoever had been chasing her during the storm hadn't circled back and finished her off before the rescue teams could arrive? Was her cousin why the attack at the hotel had failed? Why the threat hadn't come until after her daughter was out of the building?

Sam had avoided Luca so many times since being relocated. She'd been lucky, no matter how she'd tempted fate.

Oh, Carlos...

Of course Luca would have wanted to get his affairs in order, once he hit town. She didn't put it past her brother to have known all along that Carlos couldn't be trusted to finish her off. Luca would have enjoyed allowing their cousin to dig his own grave, while Luca waited to make an example of Carlos when it would achieve maximum impact.

"Are you okay?" Randy asked.

"Are we clear what happens when we get to the physicians' center?" Max pressed before she could answer. "My people cover every move that's made once we hit Atlanta. The only way I can guarantee your safety is if—"

"We hand over the baby, then sit there with targets on our chests while you neutralize the threat to Sam's and my daughter's lives," Randy finished for him. "I think that's clear enough."

Momentarily satisfied, Max nodded for the agent beside him to head out. Their black SUV cleared the lodge's parking lot. Their entourage drove toward the adjoining rural highway—a matching SUV in front of them, with two more falling in line behind.

"The target is Luca," Max reminded them, "not just whichever poor bastard he has riding shotgun, or whoever my team's damn leak turns out to be. We bring Luca down, and the Montgomery family gets their lives back. If we don't—"

"You can't promise any of us will ever be safe." Sam sat straighter.

She bit her lip until her eyes watered. The sting of it was oddly centering. Blinking back her tears, she glanced up at Randy's face. His expression was set. Determined. Her invincible rescue hero was in this to win it. To win her.

"Look at what he did to Carlos," she said. "If Lucas ever gets to you and your family—"

"He won't." Randy kissed the tip of her nose. "Not after today."

She tried to believe him. She tried to focus on fighting for them and their daughter instead of fighting against Luca. Or not fighting at all and running again.

This was her last chance to have the life she'd

always wanted for her and Gabby. She wasn't going to let her brother take her dreams away again.

THE ELEVATOR PINGED on the fifth floor of the physicians' center. The doors whooshed open. A wave of déjà vu rolled over Randy.

A few days ago, he'd stumbled across a similar threshold next door at Atlanta Memorial, wondering who the hell Sam was and if he'd ever get the chance to ask her. This morning, the mother of his child was at his side, carrying a newborn-sized doll and ignoring the pain and exhaustion caused by simply being on her feet.

They were fighting together now. Making something real out of the half lives they'd been living. So why did it feel as if he was about to lose Sam forever, just like it had a week ago?

She'd been skittish all morning, after the promises they'd made each other last night. She'd grown more distant since hearing about her cousin's murder. Randy hadn't pushed her to talk about it. But he *was* going to hear her say she loved him. He was going to hear their daughter's name on her lips. He wasn't going to stop fighting until their future was something Sam could believe in.

They walked onto the floor. The soothing whir of a vending machine snagged his attention.

"I'll be damned."

A replica of the battered beast at the hospital— what had Kate called it? Herbie?—occupied an alcove to the left of the elevator. Randy glared at the evil clone and kept walking. He was thirsty as hell. He hadn't made time for breakfast. But Randy and Sam had been instructed not to draw undue attention to themselves. Which meant Randy couldn't vent his growing frustration by pummeling a stingy pile of junk that would no doubt deny him one of the few luxuries he indulged in.

Dean and two of his deputies led Randy and Sam to the office where they were to wait. A bubble of security had been not-so-discreetly positioned outside the windowless room. The interior placement of the office was supposed to guarantee Randy and Sam could be monitored from every access point, no matter how vulnerable they needed to appear for the sting to work.

Randy turned into the office with Sam, and came face-to-face with the reality that she wasn't the only person on scene that Dean's people had better keep safe.

"You look like you could use this, big boy," Kate said in an awful Mae West impersonation.

She held out a Yoo-hoo that was so cold, condensation dripped down the sides. Randy took the can, then pulled Kate into an uncharacteristic hug that startled her at first. Then she was hugging him back.

"This is a really bad idea," he said into her ear.

He didn't want his friends anywhere near the danger heading for him and Sam. He stepped back and held out his hand to shake with the man standing beside Kate.

"Thank you for taking such a personal interest in

our daughter's case." He squeezed just a littler harder than necessary.

Seth Washington winced, but his expression remained all business.

Kate took the swaddled doll from Sam.

"You're a local hero, Lieutenant Montgomery," Seth said. "The hospital board is pleased to offer your daughter our very best care." His smile was understanding and genuine as he turned to Sam. "If you and your security detail will just wait here, I'll personally insure that you're updated as soon as your baby's condition can be determined."

"We'll be able to see her then?" Sam asked on cue. She sounded suitably terrified. "I know it will take time for you to finish your work, and I understand why we have to stay here instead of going with her. But if there's any way I could check in on her—"

"We'll take good care of her." Kate tucked the blanket tighter around the doll. "And we'll get word to you about her condition as soon as we can."

Max had said key staff would play along for the sake of whomever might be watching. Luca had to believe that this *emergency* trip back to Atlanta General was his last shot to get to Sam. Randy should have guessed that Kate and Seth would invite themselves along for the ride.

"Your daughter may need to be sedated for some of the procedures," Seth explained. "Once the diagnostics are run, we'll monitor her until she's awake. We'll have to be confident her respiration has stabilized before she can be released."

"How long will that take?" Sam wilted into a nearby chair, her exhaustion real and testing Randy's commitment to play along with this farce.

She was grieving her cousin and terrified of her brother. And she was genuinely worried about their daughter. They both were. Max had relayed news on the ride in that their baby had been breathing well enough to be released from her regional hospital. She and Randy's family would be on their way to a pediatric center in Charlotte soon, so further testing could be done.

"Dr. Washington will check back with you." Kate's professional smile turned indulgent when Randy popped the Yoo-hoo's top and chugged it. "I need to get her over to the hospital."

"We'll be right here." Randy thanked her with a nod. "Both of you be careful..." He caught Max Dean's warning glance. "Be careful with our daughter."

Seth nodded, worry clouding his normally clear gaze. He and Kate left. Randy sat and took Sam's hand.

There was nothing left to do but wait.

God, he hated waiting.

"I should be with her," Sam said.

"She's in good hands," he reminded them both. "We're doing the right thing."

His stare bored holes in the back of Dean's head. The marshal had posted himself in the office's wide doorway, legs braced apart and hands clasped behind his back. He never stopped scanning up and down the hall.

"We're doing the only thing we can do," Sam argued. "That doesn't make it right."

"It'll be right when it works."

And it was going to work, as long as Sam stayed with him. Believed in him. If she was strong enough to face down her brother's threats, she was strong enough to love Randy.

"This is the way through," he assured Sam. "The first thing you learn in fire school—there's always a way through. You just have to pick a direction, adjust as needed and keep fighting until you're out."

Sam leaned against his shoulder. The weight of her was almost nonexistent, as if she was already gone. To anyone walking by, they would look like exactly what they were supposed to be—a couple united and supporting each other while they waited for news about their sick baby.

"You can't bull your way through everything, Randy," she said. "I get it. It's how you've survived. It's why you're so good at saving people. You never let fear win. You never doubt yourself. And I admire you for still being able to believe like that, after what you and your family went through. I want you to teach our daughter how to do that. But maybe…"

"No maybe." He stroked her hair. "I'm right here. I'm not leaving your side. We'll get through this together."

You never let the fear win…

Randy frowned as the terror of losing the only woman he'd ever loved crept closer.

CHAPTER SEVENTEEN

"MAYBE THIS ISN'T..." Luca's driver started to say, then he stopped. Frowned. Hesitated.

They'd just pulled into the alley on the west side of Atlanta Memorial's new physicians' center.

"Maybe this isn't what?" Luca asked.

Danny was a good kid. Luca had been grooming him for years. He'd flown him in from New York as soon as he'd known there'd be blood in Atlanta. Danny was usually all smiles. Luca liked that about him. Carlos had been like that once.

"Maybe this isn't the best time to go after your sister," the stocky twentysomething said.

"What are you thinking?"

Danny was one of Luca's best guns. He'd earned that position through grit, intuition, attention to detail and loyalty. And, he'd never met Sam, so there were no questions about whether he'd hesitate to take her out if it came to that.

"I'm thinking they know we're coming, so we shouldn't be coming." Danny pulled his gun and checked the clip.

"They don't know how we're coming." Which

gave Luca the element of surprise, while the target was overconfident.

"They know you don't have a choice."

"Everyone knows I don't have a choice. My enemies, especially. Makes this a nondecision. I take Sam out. No more middlemen. No more waiting. I clean up my family's mess today, while everyone's watching."

"She didn't come back for her little sister when you asked her to?" Danny holstered his automatic. "What kind of cold-hearted bitch does that?"

"The kind that doesn't respect family." Luca had forbidden Sam to marry. She'd been too young. Too impressionable. Her pursuing that relationship after he'd called her off would have damaged him, and he'd had to end it. Her fault, not his. But she'd always blamed him for everything, even when they were kids. "My sister's never understood what our family's about—we protect one another, no matter what, or our enemies will pick us off one by one."

"She's always wanted out?" Danny clearly couldn't comprehend it.

"Nobody but my father could ever reason with her. Once he was gone, she became more and more rebellious."

"And now?"

"Now my sister's baby's in jeopardy, and she finally understands what it's like to have no choice. She has her responsibility to the family she'd chosen to create, just as I do to mine. It's taken two years, but I've finally got her."

CHARLIE WAS JUST ABOUT DONE hiding and waiting.

Something was off. He could feel it. Same way he could tell when a routine call was about to blow up in his ladder company's face.

Something was in the air—danger, waiting for its chance to unleash. Rick's contacts had confirmed that the hospital's half-constructed physicians' center would be ground zero. Which had told Charlie exactly where he needed to be if he was going to get into the mix and help his brother. There was one man even the feds would have to go through, if they wanted to turn anything related to Atlanta Memorial into a carefully contained battleground.

But where the hell was—

The door opened to the shadowy office Charlie was waiting in. A tall figure wearing a lab coat walked in, absently flipping the light.

"It's about damn time," Charlie said before the man had time to look up from the PDA he was typing into.

Seth Washington skidded to a halt, then did a double take.

"Holy Hell!" He shut the door behind him. "You've got to be kidding me."

"Does it look like I'm kidding?" Charlie threw himself into the love seat across from Seth's desk.

He braced his forearms on his knees and stared down the older man. Not all that much older. But looking at the dark circles and frown lines marring Seth's pretty-boy face, no one would have known he and Charlie could have gone to high school together. Not that they really had. Seth Washington swam in

Atlanta's private school circles. The Montgomerys had always lived on the other side of the social tracks.

"You look—" Seth slapped his PDA to his desk and shucked out of his lab coat "—like you're raring for a fight."

"Only if Randy needs me."

"He needs you to be with the rest of your family and his sick child, making sure there are no problems there."

"Rick and Chris have Emma and Jessie and the baby covered. That asshole Gianfranco is targeting my kid brother here—so here's where I am."

"Do I want to know how—" Seth started to ask.

"How I know what I know? How I got here? Who cares? How are the feds and the APD and whoever else is involved going to keep my brother safe? That's all that matters. Randy could have been killed yesterday. Emma and I and the baby could have been caught in that blast. The woman my kid brother loves is a moving target, and he won't leave her side until this is settled."

"And?" Seth demanded, his expression giving nothing away.

He and Rick Downing had gone a few rounds together not too long ago, and Seth had held his own. The good doctor, pressed pants and pedigreed education and all, wasn't someone Charlie would have chosen to tangle with. But nothing about this situation was giving him a choice.

"And you're going to tell me where they are and what the plan is," he challenged. "I swear, I'll stay out of the way unless there's a problem. But if there is—"

"You'll what? Their location is secured. Guarded

at every entrance. No civilians will be endangered. No one the feds don't want on that floor is going to get anywhere near Randy and Sam."

"I can go anywhere I want to in this place, as long as you're leading the way."

"And why the hell would I do that?"

"Because you never play by the rules when it comes to protecting people you care about, any more than my family does." The doctor had a rebellious streak Charlie had admired for years. "Dean has a leak in his team. Maybe more than one person feeding Luca information. You mean to tell me you don't think it's possible that Gianfranco can penetrate their protection. Again. I—"

The building shook, followed immediately by the sound of a not-so-distant explosion. The lights flickered on and off, then held.

Shit!

Seth was pulling his lab coat back on.

Charlie stood and waited for the already moving doctor to lead the way out of his office.

CHAPTER EIGHTEEN

SAM CLUNG to Randy as the world rocked around them. The fire alarms were blaring. People were screaming. The familiar nightmare of it was closing in. They'd dropped to the office floor. Darkness had descended on their windowless room almost immediately after the explosion.

From the hallway, a disembodied voice had yelled for them to stay put. That they'd be safe there until an armed escort was ready to evacuate them. Beyond that, no one was telling them anything. It had probably only been a few minutes. But lying beneath Randy with her entire body aching and the lingering smell of smoke wafting in from the hallway, it felt that hours had passed.

"Was it a bomb?" She tried to sit up.

"Stay down." Randy pressed his body more firmly against her. "Let's wait until—"

An electronic buzzing heralded a splash of green emergency lighting, flickering from the exit sign just outside the office door. Artificial light stuttered, then it held. Sam could see shadows moving in the hallway now. A haze of smoke shifting from waist-level up. She should have been reassured that Max's team was out there, protecting her. Except they'd wanted her brother to find them. The leak in Sam's protections had done what it was supposed to do. The threat was closing in.

"That might just be dust from an explosion, right?" Sam asked, as if it would somehow be better for parts of the building to be floating around their fifth floor hallway, rather than smoke.

"It's not dust." Randy finally allowed her to sit.

Her always-under-control fireman was tense. Looking around. Listening.

"Luca won't get this far," he assured her.

"You don't know him. *They* don't know him. He's—"

"He's doing exactly what the guys in the suits want him to."

"In a burning building?"

"There's a fire." Randy ran his hands down her arm. "Doesn't mean the building's burning. We're only a hundred feet from the stairwell. That's our fireproof way out if we need one."

"Exactly the sort of reasoning Luca would be banking on."

"Which is probably why Max hasn't moved us yet."

"So, we're trapped?"

"No, we're waiting. Together." Randy kissed her, his confidence and his touch drawing her to him even now.

Especially now.

"But—" Shots rang out from the direction of the elevators. "Luca!"

"Okay." Randy winced in apology as he pulled her IV free. He kissed away her cry of pain. He helped her up. "Now, we're moving."

"YOU TWO HEAD BACK down those stairs," an APD officer barked on the stairwell landing outside the physicians' center's fifth floor. "This is a restricted area, and you're not authorized—"

Charlie and Seth stopped, but they weren't leaving.

"I'm the chief of staff of this hospital," Seth said. "I'm authorized to go anywhere I damn well please in this place, and you know it." He nodded his head Charlie's way. "This is one of Atlanta's top firemen. We're inspecting every floor of my hospital's new physicians' center after the explosion. As quietly as possible, of course, but we're doing it."

The cop shook his head.

"This area is off-limits to unauthorized personnel, sir. We've already killed two men trying to rush the floor since the explosion."

Seth crossed his arms. "In return for permitting this operation to take place, I was promised access to any part of the center at any time. That was the hospital board's stipulation."

"Besides—" Charlie stepped onto the landing and checked out the officer's nameplate "—Officer Lewis. You just said you'd secured things."

Lewis's hand went to a communications device curled around his ear. "We've contained the stairwell, yes. The visitors' elevators have been cleared, too."

"You mean the elevators some maniac trashed

fifteen minutes ago?" Seth joined Charlie. "The board wants a report—from me. Now. My ass is on the line for agreeing to this fiasco. You either let us on the floor, or I signal an evacuation of the entire place. Your people will have no choice but to pack it in."

"I…" Lewis hesitated, then reached for the hands-free walkie-talkie attached to the shoulder of his uniform. "I need backup to cover the stairwell." To Charlie and Seth, he added, "I can't let you two advance unescorted, Dr. Washington."

Footsteps thundered toward them from below. Lewis drew his weapon and stepped around them, his gun raised and trained down the stairwell. When another officer rounded the flight below them, Lewis turned back. He didn't reholster his weapon.

"Stay down and against the wall," he said. "Don't get yourself or me shot and make me regret doing this. My ass is officially on the same line as yours now."

Lewis approached the door leading from the stairwell to the fifth floor. Charlie and Seth shared a silent stare.

"All eyes," the officer said into his walkie-talkie. "Stairwell door opening. Repeat, I'm entering through the stairwell. Two parties in tow."

A squawk of chatter Charlie couldn't decode must have cleared them through.

"Wait here." Lewis opened the door with his free hand and caught it with his foot. He positioned his gun through the gap. The officer who'd reached the landing beside Seth and Charlie covered their backsides. When Lewis nodded his head, the other officer grabbed the door. Lewis stepped through. He scanned one direction with his eyes and weapon, then the other.

"Clear," he said.

The other officer motioned for Seth and Charlie to follow his partner.

Seth and Charlie stepped onto the floor.

The stairwell door closed soundlessly behind them.

RANDY SHIFTED Sam behind his back as they neared the office's door. His arm braced her, protected her, while he put his body between her and whatever was happening in the hall. His hand itched to be holding the handgun he'd given back to Dean yesterday.

Another blast of gunfire rang out. Hell if he could tell where it was coming from, or see through the hazy gloom. All he was certain of was that their sting had just gone from a bad idea to a disaster, progressing exactly as planned. They'd drawn Luca Gianfranco out. The mobster was there to finish things with Sam. Job well done.

"Randy?" Sam shivered behind him. "Max said to wait here until—"

"I'm not going to wait for you to be picked off by your brother or whoever he's gotten to betray Dean's team."

Enough of sitting and doing nothing. Enough waiting and watching. His commitment was to Sam, not this insane plan.

"It's Luca," she said. "He's—"

"He's blown the compressor for the central elevators." A familiar shadow suddenly loomed in the doorway.

"Get out of my way." Randy challenged Sam's federal marshal.

More gunshots echoed from too nearby.

"Get down." Dean yanked hard on Randy's arm.

He didn't loosen his hold until Randy and Sam were kneeling beside him. Max motioned with his gun. The agents accompanying him closed ranks, effectively flanking the doorway. A female agent that Randy recognized but couldn't place joined the group.

"Are you two out of your minds moving around?" Dean demanded. "We can't secure you outside this room, and—"

"That's what my brother does best." Sam coughed. "He corners people where they think they're safest. He has to know our location by now, and he'll—"

"My men have every access point to this floor covered." Dean fingered the comm device at his ear.

"So will Luca's people," Sam argued.

"We have it covered," insisted the female agent— Glinda, Randy finally remembered. Her hand was at her own comm device. Her frown matched her boss's as they listened to whatever information was pouring in from their team.

"Is that what the gunfire means?" Randy flinched as another shot rang out. "Yeah, you've got our asses covered but good! It's time to get Sam out. She's done her job. Her safety comes first. You either give us your exit plan, or I'm getting her out myself."

"Which will put her at even more risk," Dean assured him.

Randy grabbed Sam's hand. He fought for focus. To remember how he'd asked *her* to be strong enough to see this through. Now Sam was the one calmly facing reality, while Randy wanted to take Dean apart with his bare hands. This was how Sam got her life back. She was watching him, waiting for him to decide. Trusting him to stand by her.

Randy closed his eyes. Told himself to trust the team fighting around him. Just like at an accident scene, where his job was to set a rescue plan in motion, then turn things over to his men. Except what he'd turned over to Sam was his heart, and now he had to trust Max Dean with protecting it.

"I love you," he reminded her before turning back to her protection detail.

"Tell me what your next move is," he demanded. "No more need-to-know. How are you going to protect Sam from her brother?"

Dean was still listening to the reports streaming into his earpiece.

"The fire's contained in the basement," he reported, "though there's smoke still circulating through the central elevator shafts. Armed suspects were neutralized on the ground floor just after the blast." His hand dropped from his ear. He gave Randy and Sam his undivided attention for the first time. "This has all the earmarks of someone trying to herd a mark into a trap. Which means we can't remove Sam without giving Luca Gianfranco the chance to eliminate her. He's trying to flush her out."

"My brother was probably already on this floor before his men took out the compressors," Sam said. "He's sitting back somewhere, watching the fallout from his attack. Luca likes to show up early for a party—my father taught him that. He'd want the best vantage point, while he waited for his opening."

Dean didn't seem particularly surprised by Sam's assessment. Randy tucked her closer against him.

"Is that a possibility?" he asked.

"That someone's put Gianfranco in position, maybe even before you arrived? It's entirely possible. Even more reason to not deviate from our plan and make half-assed emotional mistakes."

"Your plan is bullshit, *Marshal* Dean," Randy yelled over the screeching alarms. "What about us being window dressing?"

"Plans change," Dean said. "And I've arranged for contingencies that weren't shared with my chain of command."

"Which are?"

"There are staff elevators diagonally opposite the central ones," Glinda said. "For bringing over patients from the hospital for consults. They don't stop on all floors, and they won't be officially operational until the construction is completed."

"Please tell me they're *unofficially* working well enough to use." Randy took his first full breath since the explosion, then coughed over the bite of smoke.

"They are," Dean confirmed. "No one but me and my deputies know. The staff elevators work on different compressors than the central banks. I've secured an auxiliary room on the garden basement floor for Sam, just in case."

"Auxiliary room?" Sam asked.

"Somewhere to stash you, if we couldn't get you all the way out. At this point we have to assume that Luca is monitoring every exit. We need to appear to be trying to evacuate you from the building via a more traditional route, meanwhile I'll be securing you five flights down until your brother's in custody."

"Okay, 007," Sam sassed. She gave a shaky smile, and Randy couldn't resist kissing her again. "How does this work?"

"We split the two of you up," Dean said. "I only have four deputies, so it will be tight, but…" His hand went back to his ear. He cursed under his breath, then sighed and shot Randy a rueful smile. "Actually, Lieutenant Montgomery, your troublesome family may just have made my day."

"What the hell are you—"

Randy didn't get to finish his question before a crouching APD officer escorted two other stooped figures into the dimly lit room. Then Seth Washington and Charlie were straightening to their full heights beside him.

"What the hell are you doing here?"

"Doing what's best for your daughter," Charlie said, "just like I promised. And what's best is for you and

Sam to get out of this in one piece, so that little girl can grow up with both parents, the way she deserves."

Randy swallowed the curse he'd been about to fling at his big brother. Instead, he found himself hauling Charlie into a hug that included Sam.

Family. It's what Randy and his brothers and sister had always been fighting for. It's what they'd never given up on. Randy felt a renewed surge of confidence that no weapon could give him.

Dean eyed them. "Why do I get the feeling this isn't going to bode well for my career?"

"Is your career what we're most concerned about at the moment?" Charlie asked.

"No." Dean nodded. "How do you feel about duck hunting?"

"Duck hunting?" Randy sputtered.

"You and Charlie here are about to become decoys." Dean nodded to Glinda who'd stepped past Randy and Sam and further into the office. The female agent began stripping out of her suit jacket and pants, ignoring Randy and Charlie as if they weren't there.

"Decoys?" Randy asked Dean.

"I'm with you," Glinda chimed in. "While I play the part of Ms. Gianfranco here, Sam goes with Marshal Dean."

"Dr. Washington," Dean said to Seth. "You'll need to stay here. But hand your lab coat to your partner in crime."

Seth took off his coat while Glinda began passing her clothes to Sam.

"Do we have to split up?" Sam's grip on Randy's hand felt like a vise. She stared up at him. "Luca will think I'm with you still. He'll be gunning for you."

Nodding, forcing himself to function, Randy began to gently remove the sling from her arm. Then he went to work on the buttons of Sam's dress.

"It's the best way to draw out your brother while Dean gets you out," he said. "It ends this."

"No!" Sam batted his fingers away.

Randy went back to work on the buttons without comment.

"You're not…" Sam grabbed his hands. "I can't—"

"Yes, you can." Randy's palms were sweating and his hands were shaking at the thought of leaving someone else to protect her.

His fingers slipped trying to work the next button. He couldn't lose Sam. He'd never survive it. He pulled her close, holding on to her for a few endless seconds. Then he told himself to get a grip. To do what he'd promised her he would. Shuddering, dying inside, he moved her away.

"Damn it, Sam. I believe in you. I believe you love me and our daughter enough to get through whatever craziness Dean has planned." Randy set her further away from him. "Your protection detail knows what they're doing. Trust them. Trust me. I know you can do this, baby."

Randy held his breath, willing Sam to fight for them. For the family he wanted to build with her. No more running. No more hiding. This was it. He didn't like it any more than she did. But if Sam was going to make it out of this alive, Randy had to let her go, and trust her to come back to him.

Nodding at the conviction he'd forced into his expression, Sam slowly began to undress herself.

"All right." Randy smiled down into her terrified gaze.

He'd never been more proud of anyone. God, please, don't let him be making the biggest mistake of his life. She'd slipped away from him in Savannah. He wouldn't survive losing her now.

"Let's hear your can't-lose plan for digging our asses out of this mess," he said to Dean. "Then, let's get it on."

Max Dean chuckled, nodding. "Let's get it on."

LUCA HAD SMILED when the charges his men had set beside the elevator compressors went off. Next had come the blare of the fire alarms, followed by the distant racket of gunfire, as two of Luca's more expendable men distracted the APD officers they'd been told would be staking out the ground floor. All while Luca sat waiting, cramped, in a tiny room where no one would be looking for him.

He was biding his time, giving his sister and her handlers space to take the bait. Enough time for the federal marshals to decide to get her off the fifth floor. A knock on the supply room's door announced Danny's arrival.

"They're on the move," Danny said. "It's time."

Luca opened up, only a crack until he could

confirm that Danny was alone. Then he stood, securing his weapon.

"Everything's in place. Sam's protection detail will be attempting to evacuate her any minute now," Danny assured him.

"Then let's add a touch of excitement to their trip." It was thrilling, how much Sam still underestimated him. How much the feds did.

The sacrifices Luca made every day would have protected and cared for Sam and Gabby forever, if Sam had only trusted him. But the little bitch had been too weak to do even that.

"I don't care what happens to anyone else," he reminded Danny over the blare of the alarms still clamoring through the building. "But my sister's mine to deal with."

CHAPTER NINETEEN

RANDY WALKED toward the central elevators with his brother and the others in his detail. He held the feminine hand clutched in his as if he'd never let it go, playing his role for all he was worth. Meanwhile, Max and Sam and the one deputy Max had taken with them were walking in the opposite direction, as if they were merely a team of agents scanning the fifth floor and other parts of the building for unseen threats.

You can do this, Sam.

"Turn at the central elevators," Charlie said. "Stay behind your cover, and—"

"I've got the plan," Randy snarled at his big brother. "You're nuts for involving yourself in this. When I said take care of the baby, I meant just that. I don't need—"

"You're distracted as hell," Charlie growled back. "You have been since the accident. Since St. Patrick's Day. You need someone besides these feds covering your ass. And that someone is me. Deal with it."

"What the hell good do you think you're going to be if we do attract enough attention to get Sam out safely. There are five armed professionals surrounding me, and—"

"And none of them are your family. No one's going to cover you the way I will. Not even the good witch here."

"Who?" The woman at Randy's side glared at his brother.

"Glinda, the good witch," Charlie explained.

Randy snorted as the deputy's grip tightened painfully.

"Don't look at me." Charlie was all innocence. "Emma's the one who started calling her that. The point is—"

Shots rang out as they neared the central elevators. The two male deputies and two APD officers completing their party blurred into motion, weapons drawn, turning in a single motion toward the hallway to their left.

"Get down!" Charlie positioned his body in front of Randy and Glinda.

What happened next took only seconds. Their team fired back. Another barrage of gunfire returned. The fire alarm continued to blare around them. Glinda dragged Charlie down.

"Shit!" Charlie gasped as they both collapsed to the floor.

"Charlie!" Randy wrapped his arms around his brother.

"Behind here." Glinda pulled at Randy's arm.

He dragged his brother behind the vending machine. Charlie was wheezing. Coughing.

"Damn, man," Randy cursed once they were reasonably protected. "You weigh a ton! You better not be dying on me, you got that?"

"Shut the hell up and help me get this thing off," his brother bit out.

Randy yanked open Seth's lab coat, then pulled up his brother's T-shirt. Bullets pinged into the vending machine. More shots were fired from Dean's men, who were giving as good as they got. Randy just prayed it was Luca they were wrangling with, and that they finished the psychotic bastard off.

He stared down at the bullet-proof vest Dean's men had produced for Charlie to wear. Randy had donned an identical one. A bullet was embedded in his brother's protective gear. Nothing seemed to have penetrated. No blood anywhere.

"Damn, man." Randy covered his eyes with his hand. His fingers were shaking. "Just…damn."

Vest or not, Charlie had put himself between Randy and the madness closing in on them. And the shooting wasn't over yet. Dean's team was doing their job—keeping their attackers engaged.

Would it be enough for Sam to reach the hospital elevators? Would she be able to handle the sound of everything crashing down around them? Randy peeked around the vending machine, across the floor in the direction Dean and Sam had headed out. A bullet banked off the metal just above his head.

"Stay down!" Glinda yanked him back. "Keep your head down, you idiot."

"Get me an update on Sam," he demanded. "Or I'm—"

"Your ass isn't doing anything but staying here." Charlie shoved Randy further into the corner while Glinda tuned into the comm device in her ear. "Sam's got her own protection, and—"

"And who knows if this charade is doing any good. I—"

"You're not going to get yourself killed," Glinda chimed in. "Stick with the plan. Trust my team to do their jobs."

"I'll trust them, as soon as you get me the information that Sam made it off this floor."

"Kiss the baby for me, if—" Sam had started to say when they'd split up.

"You'll kiss her yourself," Randy had insisted.

"But if I don't—"

"You'll make it out of this, Sam. I know it."

There'd been doubt in her brave smile as they'd broken into two teams. There'd been something too close to goodbye in their final kiss.

"We're clear," Glinda announced.

"What?" Randy and Charlie asked in one voice.

Silence resonated. Glinda was on her feet. They followed her lead and stepped into the hallway. The rest of their detail was still on point, watching. But the showdown was over.

"Nix the alarms," Glinda said into her comm link, "and flip the switch."

The deafening blare of the fire alarms was

squelched at the same moment that the auxiliary lighting flickered off and the mains came back on.

"There was never a problem with the power?" Charlie asked.

"It kind of added something to the effect—" Sam's stand-in smirked. "Don't ya think?"

"Where's Gianfranco?" Randy wanted to know.

There were two bodies on the floor down the hall. Someone from the decoy team knelt beside them. The APD officer looked back, shaking his head and frowning, then headed further down the hallway, checking and clearing each office he passed. He touched a hand to his ear and began talking.

"That was too close," Charlie said. "Is Luca Gianfranco dead?"

"He's not here." Glinda was listening to her teammates' reports. "There's—"

"What do you mean he's not here?" Randy rounded on her, backing her up against the bullet-shredded vending machine.

"Gianfranco sent his own decoy." Glinda nodded toward the two downed men. "That's one of our APD contingent and one of our own guys."

"One of your deputies?"

Glinda winced. "It explains how Luca found the hotel yesterday. How he got into this building."

"So where is he now? If you didn't draw him out with this dog and pony show, where's the man who's trying to kill your federal witness?"

"We're working on it."

"Is he tracking Sam?"

"We don't know. We're—"

"Working on it," Randy parroted back, allowing her to step away to confer with her team. "Yeah."

Just like they'd been working on keeping Sam alive for two years.

"No word from Dean?" he asked

"They're still on the move. He'll report in when Ms. Gianfranco's secure."

Randy checked his watch.

It had been less than five minutes since they'd split up.

"She's going to be okay, man," Charlie said beside him. He'd bent at the waist and was rubbing his chest beneath the Kevlar vest. He was still having trouble breathing. "You've done…everything you can. It's out of your hands now. You have to believe that she's going to be okay."

"Like we believed Mom would make it back to us alive?" Randy asked.

Charlie blinked at the reminder. Randy slammed his fist into the vending machine that, unlike Herbie on the pediatric floor, seemed to have taken a liking to him. With a whirring clunk a can hissed from the bowels of the thing. A frosty Yoo-hoo sat in the dispenser.

"Look at that, man," Charlie said with a tight laugh. "This must be your lucky day."

Except Randy had talked Sam into this crazy plan. He'd talked her into believing this would work. And if he'd been wrong? Nothing in his life would ever be right again. Not the career Randy had lived for. Not even returning to his own family—the people who'd protected him and kept him sane since they were kids.

Randy needed Sam *and* their daughter.

He needed the hope that poured through him whenever he thought of the future they could build.

"Yeah." He picked up the can and popped the top. When he gulped down the smooth, frosty chocolate, all he could taste was fear. "I'm a lucky man…"

"ALMOST THERE," Max said.

Sam nodded. She was scared out of her mind. But she was determined to make the most out of this chance Randy and the rest of Max's team were giving her. She kept moving.

Shots had erupted behind them, while Max and another deputy got Sam to the staff elevator and off the floor. They hadn't received a report from their team by the time the elevators had opened to the garden basement. Now Max's transmissions were being garbled from some kind of interference. No news on the outcome of the decoy. No confirmation that Luca had been contained.

The ground floor basement level was vacant, its construction nowhere near finished. No furnishings. No partitions. Just winding hallways currently illuminated by the ambient light shining through floor-to-ceiling windows that comprised the floor's outer wall. Max hadn't activated any lights when they'd left the elevator. He wasn't certain they were the only ones there.

They passed office after office, some with doors, some merely empty shells yet to be tended to. Max and his deputy and Sam maneuvered through a maze of walls lined with plastic and half-formed Sheetrock. A wall was always to Sam's left. Max stayed to the right and no more than half a step ahead. His deputy covered Sam's back.

Max kept touching the device at his ear, trying to get a report. How much attention had the other team drawn? Had anyone been hurt in the gunfire? Randy? Charlie?

They rounded another corner, Max taking point and sweeping the hallway first. He suddenly stopped, his hand to his ear. Something was finally getting through. His deepening frown wasn't encouraging.

Sam didn't push for details, and not just because distracting the men protecting her could get them all dead. If the disturbing report was about Randy, she couldn't bear to hear it now.

They headed out again.

"Just one more hallway." Max held up a hand as they approached the next corner, the same as he had with each of the others.

They stopped. The deputy covered behind them while Max scanned the next hall with his gun. He gave his silent *Clear* signal. Sam and the other deputy moved to make the turn.

Gunfire erupted.

"Get down!" Max yelled.

The deputy pulled Sam to the floor. A chunk of the wall where her head had been exploded.

"Stay down!" The deputy kept a hand on her back, the pressure against her injured shoulder excruciating.

More gunfire.

A thud on the ground beside her.

"I'm hit!" Max gasped.

Sam lifted her head to see.

"Stay down!" the other marshal repeated. "How bad?"

"Arm. Near the shoulder." Max's voice sounded more pissed than anything. "I can move. There's more than one. Two, possibly three men."

"Back this way." The deputy yanked Sam to a standing position. "You take her. I'll cover for as long as I can. Get moving!"

The deputy—Sam didn't even know his name—rounded the corner and fired several shots, then pulled back, ducking while gunfire took out another chunk of the wall. Max's left arm hung limply at his side. Blood stained what she could see of the crisp shirt he wore under his jacket. With the gun still in his right hand, he motioned for Sam to head back the way they'd just come—away from the safe room no one but his immediate team was supposed to have known about.

"Someone was waiting for us down here," he said through tight lips that were white-rimmed with pain.

"Someone knew about the decoy?"

"About our backup holding location for you, at least." He motioned for Sam to take a left at the next corner—they'd come from the right when they'd passed this way the first time. "Maybe they only had backup people waiting here, just in case. Or maybe…"

"Maybe Luca's been waiting for me to come to him down here...."

"Yeah." Max pulled her to a stop. "One of my deputies has been helping him lead us around by the nose. Take this..."

He handed her his gun, then bent at the waist and sucked in several breaths.

"Max?" The Glock felt ghastly in Sam's hand, but not unfamiliar. As much as Sam despised guns, her father had trained both her and Luca how to shoot, clean and maintain them while they were still in elementary school. "Max, are you—"

"It's going to be okay." He straightened, his face dripping with sweat. He leaned into the door behind him—what looked like a conference room. "You're...you're going to be safe, Sam. I'm going to...get you back to your daughter... Back to that hulking fireman you're going to build a life with. I promise you."

His gaze swept one end of the hallway, then the other. Then he knocked three times on the door, paused, and knocked twice more. The lock turned.

Max smiled at her puzzled frown. "Luca's not the only one who hedges his bets when the stakes are high."

The door was flung open, the absence of support sending Max stumbling back into a man wearing nearly an identical suit. Only, this guy was twice Max's size, and the gun he was aiming at Sam while he kept Max from kissing the carpet was twice as ugly. The instant he recognized her, he lowered his weapon.

"Get in here before you get yourself killed." He

stepped far enough away for Sam to step inside. Leaving Max leaning against a dust-covered conference table that was only partially protected by plastic, he closed the door behind her and locked it. "And put Dean's piece away before you do something we'll both regret with it."

Pissed and shaking and pretty much convinced they were all going to die, Sam glared at the mountainous man's condescending expression and clicked the Glock's safety on without looking.

"Do something with this." She shoved the thing at him and began unbuttoning Max's jacket. "Help me get this off him."

"No…" Max jerked away from the table, nearly falling onto Sam before he caught and righted himself. "Give her back the gun, then help me—"

"Help you finish what that bullet started?" Sam demanded while he stepped around her to the door. "You can't seriously be going back out there. My brother is—"

"Going to kill us all if we just wait here." There was a grayness to Max's skin that made Sam bite back tears. He nodded to his colleague, who handed Sam back the Glock. Max pulled a second gun from a holster she hadn't seen at the small of his back. "I have no idea how long we'll be gone. No one knows about this room besides me and Fritz here. It's secure. No chance of a leak this time. Don't let anyone in unless they knock three times, wait three counts, then knock twice. Say it, so you'll remember."

Sam couldn't.

She couldn't stay here alone—waiting for Luca to kill these brave men. Wondering if he'd already taken Randy away from her, picturing what her baby's future would be like if she had to grow up with no parents to love her, once Luca found Sam and finished this. Sam shook her head, swallowing a weak, selfish sob. She didn't want to die alone. She wanted to see her child and the man she loved again.

Love...

She'd never told Randy she loved him. Now it was too late.

Max pushed away from the door, leaving a smear of blood across its surface. He covered the hand she held the gun in.

"I know I've let you down up till now," he said. "But this was our best shot at flushing out a maniac who wants you silenced. Permanently. You were brave enough to start this. Now finish it."

Max flattened his back to the wall beside the door. He nodded to Fritz, who opened the door and slipped out first, gun raised.

"Clear," the man whispered back.

"Lock up behind us," Max insisted in a similar whisper. "Tell me when you'll open it again."

Sam gulped. "Three knocks. Wait for three. Two knocks."

"Good girl." Max winked, then he was gone.

Sam lunged at the door and thumbed the insubstantial lock that wouldn't stop Luca if he got that far. She sank to the floor, the last two weeks, the last two years, careening through her mind.

You'll make it out of this, Sam. I know it.

She stared at the blood on her hands.

Randy had put everything on the line for her. He'd found some way to love her and believe in what they could have, while she'd ripped his life apart and tried to leave him and their daughter behind. She stared at Max's gun and thought of her baby girl. A baby whose future would be decided in the next few minutes.

Gunfire erupted close by. But, strangely, Sam's fear melted away. Because in that moment, she accepted that she'd do anything to not only protect her baby, but to raise her. To give her daughter a name and a future with her and Gabby. A life that wouldn't be about running from her brother's madness. A future that Randy wanted to be a part of.

She might be alone now, but Randy was waiting for her to come back to him.

The quiet outside the door dragged her attention back to the present. How long had she been sitting there? The gunfire. It had stopped. Footsteps...

Were those footsteps?

They stopped just outside.

Sam crawled backward, until she was under the conference room table. Cringing, shaking, she leveled the gun at the door and waited. Nothing happened. Not a single sound. But whoever was out there hadn't moved on.

Was it Max? His deputy?

No knock came.

Then an earsplitting blast blew out the knob and the lock and sent the door flying inward.

Sam screamed, as a looming figure filled the doorway.

"Hello, sis. Long time no see." Luca was covered in blood. Shot himself, in the chest and upper arms, he was smiling. And he was alone.

They were together again for the first time since she'd held Peter's lifeless body in her arms. Since she'd run from Luca and the life she couldn't be a part of any longer.

"What have you done?" Sam pushed to her feet, wincing at the strain on her shoulder but determined to face her brother. "Where's Randy? Where's Max?"

"I'm pretty sure your baby daddy is hanging with your ex-fiancé right about now." Luca released the clip in his automatic and snapped in a fresh one. "Swapping war stories, maybe, about how neither one of them was man enough to keep you away from me."

"Shut up." Sam felt for the safety on Max's weapon. Flipped it off. "Don't talk about them. You don't deserve to talk about them, you heartless—"

"And your federal protectors? Very clever, having a secondary exit route all mapped out, just in case this *secret* appearance of yours to care for your sick child drew me out. Nice touch with the decoy upstairs, too. Too bad I've run my own bait and switches for years. Too bad I own someone in every local and state law enforcement office within three hundred miles of here. Don't they get that I'll do whatever it takes, pay whatever it takes, to keep my sister from screwing me over to the feds? It's hell, constantly being underestimated. Especially by my own flesh and blood."

"You have no blood in your veins." Sam's right hand was shaking.

She raised her left arm, wincing at the agony in her shoulder. But she wrapped both hands around the butt of the gun. She pictured her baby's face. Then Randy's.

The pain vanished.

"You're not going to shoot your own family," Luca taunted. "You need me, Samantha. Why won't you do what I say, so you can be with Gabby and have my protection back?"

"We may share the same parents, but you're nothing to me now. And I don't need you to get Gabby back."

"When are you going to learn to stop trusting anyone but real family?"

"Monsters… Death… That's all our real family has meant to me. Lies and destruction, all for money and power and control."

Sam had finally found what she'd been looking for her entire life, nine months ago when she'd looked across a crowded street in a city she'd never been to, and watched Randy laughing with his brothers.

"Well, no worries." Luca's smile was the same as she remembered from their childhood. It was the classic Gianfranco smile their mother had said had won her over, the first time she'd met their father. "You won't have to endure being part of our monstrous family much longer."

Sam could read her death in his eyes.

"You'd really do this?" She shook the gun at him, then she dropped it to her side. Had it really come to this? One of them had to die, for the other to have the life they wanted. "You'd do this to Gabby?"

"What?" A cold-blooded murderer gazed back at her. "Would I take away the sister who's determined to tear apart the only world Gabriella's ever known? The world I can give her as the head of our family. Somehow I think she'll get over it."

Gabby, growing up with Luca teaching her. Controlling her. Sam's baby, growing up without her mother. Maybe even without her father...

Over Sam's dead body.

"You forgot one thing in your latest bait and switch, big brother."

"What's that?" Luca sounded almost indulgent.

"Me." She raised Max's gun.

Luca didn't even blink.

Why would he?

Sam had been a threat to herself all their lives, but she'd never dared challenge Luca directly. She'd wanted the safety and security of their family too much. She'd been content to let someone else call the shots. Even when she'd run to the federal prosecutor.

"You're not taking away the life I want again," she insisted.

"What life? Whoring around with some firefighter and getting yourself knocked up? Pouting in federal protection, because I wouldn't let you have Peter."

"Wouldn't let... You killed him, Luca! You killed the man I loved, while I was sleeping less than an inch away."

"I eliminated a threat to my control, just like our father taught me to." Luca's hand tightened on his weapon. "Just like I am now. It's not my fault you refuse to understand the meaning of family and loyalty."

"Oh, I understand it just fine."

Sam pointed the Glock at her brother's nonexistent heart, while she thought of Randy's mother and what Jasmine Montgomery had sacrificed so her children could live free.

"You're just not my family anymore, Luca."

They fired at the same time.

The kick from Max's Glock knocked Sam backward. Pain streaked through her shoulder.

She dropped the gun, her fingers numb, only then realizing that fire was also shooting through her chest. She glanced down at the bullet hole in her borrowed dress shirt. She lifted incredulous eyes to catch the shock mirrored in her brother's expression. Her shot had blown a hole in his chest, too, but he still held his gun.

"You bitch," he growled. He stumbled a step closer, the automatic aimed at her head this time. "You shot me? You ungrateful bi—"

Sam closed her eyes, knowing it was over.

She saw the faces of her real family one last time. Randy. Their daughter. Gabby.

I'm so sorry....

She screamed into the next roar of gunfire.

But the split second that should have passed before impact slid by her. Then another. Followed by a thud and a groan that ripped her eyes open to see

Luca crumpled at her feet—and Max sliding down the wall of the hallway outside the conference room.

She stumbled over her brother's body, making it to the hall before her legs gave out. Wilting to the floor beside Max, she reached for his gun arm, which was still raised, pointing at nothing, and pushed it to the ground.

"It's over," she said. The dimly lit hallway was fading to gray around them. "Tell me it's finally over."

"We got 'em all, Sam." Max's breathing was too fast. Too shallow. He'd been shot at least twice more. Blood was everywhere. "My people are on their way down. You and Gabby and your baby, you'll be safe."

But safe wasn't enough as the feeling of the floor beneath Sam disappeared into the gray. She wanted more, so much more.

She wanted to tell Randy she'd thought of a name for their baby....

"Randy," she said, fighting the darkness. Refusing to give in to it. "Did he make it? Is he alive? Tell him, Max... Make sure you tell him that I fought. That I believed, because I loved him. And tell him I want our daughter's name to be..."

CHAPTER TWENTY

"THEY'RE BOTH DEAD," Randy said as soon as his sister entered the well-guarded hospital room where Charlie was being checked out, despite his assurances that he was fine.

Emma was cradling Randy's sleeping daughter close. Chris followed her past the two APD officers at the door, carrying the baby's car seat. Emma stopped where Randy was sitting in a chair by the door. Chris headed for Charlie's exam table, whistling at the deep bruising mottling Charlie's chest.

Then they were all looking at Randy.

"Luca Gianfranco?" Chris asked.

"Dead," Charlie responded when Randy couldn't. "They have the body down in the morgue. Him and..."

"Sam?" Emma's eyes filled with tears.

Randy took his daughter instead of answering. Holding her soft body close was the only thing he'd felt since Glinda relayed the news that both Sam and her brother had been killed in whatever crossfire had erupted.

Seth had been in to check out Charlie's injuries and order X-rays. He'd said Max Dean was being examined a few rooms down, shot to hell but still alive, thanks to his own bulletproof vest. The APD officer and the deputy marshal who had opened fire on Randy and his decoy team were both dead, plus the man who'd gone with Dean and Sam downstairs. But Randy couldn't think past the only reality that would stick in his mind.

"They're both dead," he repeated.

Sam and Luca, what was left of the Gianfranco family, was gone. Except for Sam's sister. What would happen to Gabby now?

"I'm so sorry." Emma knelt beside him.

"You did everything you could to help her," Charlie said. "You must have really…"

"Loved her?" Randy and his brothers never talked about anything that deep. But Randy could now, because of Sam.

She'd done what she'd promised. She fought. She'd stood up to her brother and protected her baby, even though it had meant she couldn't come back to Randy. He looked down at their child.

Sam had brought his heart back to life and given him a future he'd never thought he wanted. Now, what would he do without her in it?

"I'll love her for the rest of my life." He looked from Emma's sad smile to Chris and Charlie. "I finally understand what that means, and I don't ever want to let it go. I don't want to go back to what I was before. I don't want to forget how it feels."

"You won't," Emma insisted.

His brothers nodded in agreement.

"We're here for you, man," Chris promised. "Whatever you and your baby need, you've got it."

Except what Randy and his daughter needed was Sam.

The door opened and Seth stepped in, clipboard in hand.

"They're ready for you in X-ray," he said to Charlie, "though I don't expect to find anything more serious than a cracked rib or two." Seth took in the rest of them. "One of you can head down with Charlie. Randy, why don't you bring your daughter with me, and we'll have a pediatrician check her out."

Emma and Chris had been rerouted to Atlanta, once Luca had been contained. There was no point now in taking the baby all the way to the children's hospital in Charlotte.

"We still need to get the baby in to see a specialist." Emma stepped to Charlie's side as a nurse and an orderly came in.

"First thing tomorrow," Seth promised. "But I don't want to miss anything. Let one of my staff do a quick once-over."

"We'll be back up as soon as we can," Emma said as the orderly wheeled Charlie by.

Charlie held up his hand.

The attendant stalled beside Randy.

"Thank you," Randy said, clasping his brother's hand and letting Charlie pull him into a fierce hug. "Thank you for—"

"Any time." Charlie's slap on Randy's shoulder was

weak, but familiar enough to make Randy smile. "Whatever you need, man. I'll always have your back."

Emma hugged Randy next, then ran a hand over his daughter's soft head. Randy turned back to Chris once they were gone.

"I'll be here," his brother said. "Go do what you've got to for your little girl."

Randy nodded and followed Seth into the hallway.

One of the APD officers at the door followed as they headed toward another room not far away. There were men posted there. They eyed Seth and Randy for several silent seconds before one of them opened up. Seth motioned for Randy to precede him into the room. Randy came to an abrupt halt at what waited for him inside.

There were two beds, both occupied. Max Dean was unconscious in one and hooked to about a dozen machines. In the other bed lay Sam, propped up against a pile of pillows and staring silently back at him.

RANDY WAS STANDING in the doorway, holding their daughter, staring at Sam with the same shock as when he'd walked into her hotel room.

Had it really been just yesterday?

"You're…" He stepped to the foot of her bed and stopped, as if he was afraid to believe she was really there. "You're alive?"

"She is now," Glinda said from her position just inside the door. "Up until about thirty minutes ago, Samantha Gianfranco was lying on a slab beside her brother down in the morgue. Now, it seems reports of her demise were exaggerated. Turns out she was wearing her own protective vest when her brother tried shooting a bullet straight through her heart."

"I don't understand." Randy looked from Glinda to Max, then back to Sam.

"I'm sorry," Sam said, mesmerized by the sight of Randy and their daughter. The dizziness that had sucked her under downstairs was still there. But she refused to slip into it again. Not now. "I didn't know they'd told you I was dead. Again. I..."

"She was unconscious when our people got there," Glinda explained. "She and Dean have been seen by trauma specialists, and we wouldn't tell her anything more until a few minutes ago. Max is stable and scheduled for surgery—several bullets caught him in the arms and shoulder. Sam's only bruised, thanks to her vest. But given her previous injuries, the doctors want to monitor her for a few hours. She should be fine."

"Fine?" Randy wasn't stepping closer. He wasn't reaching for her. "Why would you say she was dead, put me through that, then change the story?" He stared at Sam. "You're running again, aren't you?"

Sam didn't know what to say. When she'd come to, no one on Max's team had been telling her anything. Not even whether Randy was alive or not. Now, he and their baby were standing in front of her. And he'd been told Sam was dead?

"There's nothing to run from now," Glinda explained. "We have one of Gianfranco's men in custody. The muscle Luca had with him in the basement, some kid named Danny. He's shot to hell, and we weren't sure he would talk at first. But once he heard Gianfranco's dead, he's loosening up. Giving us everything Sam could have and more. Which means the Gianfranco organization is over, and Sam's out of the entire mess without having to testify. She's clean."

Clean. Assuming Randy could see past the trail of dead bodies and destruction she'd left in her wake. He'd just found out she was alive. And instead of holding her, he'd immediately assumed she was running—after everything she'd done to stay with him. Is that what he wanted, to finally be free of her? Had he reached his limit, now, when Glinda was telling Sam she was free of Luca?

Sam waited for him to say something. Anything.

Glinda cleared her throat.

"We'll be just outside the door," she said as she led Seth out.

Randy continued to stand there, staring.

Was it shock? Or was he trying to find a way to tell her this had all been a mistake? Facing him suddenly felt more impossible than confronting her brother had, but Sam pushed herself higher against the pillows.

"I love you," she said, not to change his mind about anything, but because he had to know. Even if it was over.

She wouldn't blame him for walking away, but she was done running. She wanted the dream, the family he'd promised her. He had to know how much.

"I think I've loved you since that morning in

Savannah, when I made myself leave. I want you to be happy, Randy. I'm sorry for all this, but I'll never be sorry that I met you, or that we had Jasmine. It will be a few months before I'm settled somewhere with Gabby. I'll understand if you don't want to, but maybe if you could come to see me then. Come to see Jasmine. Maybe we could find a way to start over. Maybe you could even find a way to love me again. Once—"

"Jasmine?" Randy finally brought their daughter closer.

Sam couldn't stop her tears from falling. But they weren't from sadness, not really. Or because he wasn't saying he loved her back. Seeing Randy looking so alive and so comfortable holding their daughter was enough. It was everything. He was going to be the best father. Sam was going to feel lucky every day that her child would grow up knowing what it was like to feel safe and loved with the Montgomerys in her life. Even if Sam could only experience it herself as an outsider.

"I want to name her Jasmine," she told him. "Your mother sacrificed everything so you could become the man you are. Because of her, you were there for me. You got me through this, when you had every right to walk away. You were what I needed to face my brother and my past and finally be free of them. I want our daughter to understand that one day, when she's old enough for you to tell her. She'll be so proud of her name, I promise. I know she will."

Randy's expression was wary, as if he was afraid of letting himself feel anything for Sam again. Then suddenly, he was leaning forward and kissing her softly, tenderly, before pulling back. Sam's tears fell as she clutched the tiny squirming body he'd left in her arms.

She stared up at Randy. At his smile.

"We'll tell her together." He braced his hands on either side of Sam and leaned forward to kiss first their daughter's head and then Sam's. "We'll give her everything she needs, together."

"Are…are you sure?"

"I can't not have you in my life, baby." His brown eyes were the warm place where Sam wanted to build her future. "When they told me you were dead, I promised myself I'd find a way to hold on, for Jasmine. Knowing you're alive will make that impossible, if I don't have you with me."

"But your family." Sam shook her head. "They must—"

"You're my family now. You're what Emma and Charlie and Chris will want for me, I assure you."

"Because of the baby?" Sam couldn't be part of damaging the magical bond Randy shared with his siblings.

"Because you brought love into my life, sweetheart. They can see that. They'll want this for me, no matter how hard it's been to get us to this point. You've taught me how to trust this need to wrap my life around someone else. No control. No guarantees. No walking away when it gets too deep. Just—"

"Now," she said with him. Was it possible? "Just today, and every other day, for as long as we have each other?"

There was a suspicious wetness in Randy's eyes now, too.

"I love you," he said. "Never doubt it, Sam. Jasmine and I will love you every day, for the rest of our lives."

* * * * *

*Harlequin Intrigue top author Delores Fossen
presents a brand-new series of
breathtaking romantic suspense!*
TEXAS MATERNITY: HOSTAGES
The first installment available May 2010:
THE BABY'S GUARDIAN

Shaw cursed and hooked his arm around Sabrina.

Despite the urgency that the deadly gunfire created, he tried to be careful with her, and he took the brunt of the fall when he pulled her to the ground. His shoulder hit hard, but he held on tight to his gun so that it wouldn't be jarred from his hand.

Shaw didn't stop there. He crawled over Sabrina, sheltering her pregnant belly with his body, and he came up ready to return fire.

This was obviously a situation he'd wanted to avoid at all cost. He didn't want his baby in the middle of a fight with these armed fugitives, but when they fired that shot, they'd left him no choice. Now, the trick was to get Sabrina safely out of there.

"Get down," someone on the SWAT team yelled from the roof of the adjacent building.

Shaw did. He dropped lower, covering Sabrina as best he could.

There was another shot, but this one came from a rifleman on the SWAT team. Shaw didn't look up, but he heard the sound of glass being blown apart.

The shots continued, all coming from his men,

which meant it might be time to try to get Sabrina to better cover. Shaw glanced at the front of the building.

So that Sabrina's pregnant belly wouldn't be smashed against the ground, Shaw eased off her and moved her to a sitting position so that her back was against the brick wall. They were close. Too close. And face-to-face.

He found himself staring right into those sea-green eyes.

How will Shaw get Sabrina out?
Follow the daring rescue and the heartbreaking
aftermath in THE BABY'S GUARDIAN
by Delores Fossen,
available May 2010 from Harlequin Intrigue.

Copyright © 2010 by Delores Fossen

HARLEQUIN® *Blaze*™

is proud to present

New York Times **bestselling author**

Vicki Lewis Thompson

with a brand-new trilogy,
SONS OF CHANCE
**where three sexy brothers
meet three irresistible women.**

Look for the first book
WANTED!

*Available beginning in June 2010
wherever books are sold.*

---

red-hot reads

www.eHarlequin.com

HB79548

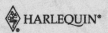

HARLEQUIN®

INTRIGUE®

BESTSELLING
HARLEQUIN INTRIGUE® AUTHOR

DELORES
FOSSEN

PRESENTS AN ALL-NEW
THRILLING TRILOGY

TEXAS MATERNITY:
HOSTAGES

When masked gunmen take over the maternity ward
at a San Antonio hospital, local cops, FBI and the scared
mothers can't figure out any possible motive. Before
long, secrets are revealed, and a city that has been on
edge since the siege began learns the truth behind the
negotiations and must deal with the fallout.

LOOK FOR

THE BABY'S GUARDIAN, *May*
DEVASTATING DADDY, *June*
THE MOMMY MYSTERY, *July*

www.eHarlequin.com   HI69472

Bestselling Harlequin Presents® author

Lynne Graham

introduces

VIRGIN ON HER WEDDING NIGHT

Valente Lorenzatto never forgave Caroline Hales's
abandonment of him at the altar. But now he's
made millions and claimed his aristocratic Venetian
birthright—and he's poised to get his revenge.
He'll ruin Caroline's family by buying out their
company and throwing them out of their mansion…
unless she agrees to give him the wedding night
she denied him five years ago.…

**Available May 2010
from Harlequin Presents!**

www.eHarlequin.com

HP12915

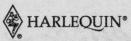

LAURA MARIE ALTOM

The Baby Twins

Stephanie Olmstead has her hands full raising
her twin baby girls on her own. When she runs
into old friend Brady Flynn, she's shocked to find
herself suddenly attracted to the handsome airline
pilot! Will this flyboy be the perfect daddy—
or will he crash and burn?

"LOVE, HOME & HAPPINESS"

www.eHarlequin.com

HAR75309

Former bad boy Sloan Hawkins is back in Redemption, Oklahoma, to help keep his aunt's cherished garden thriving and to reconnect with the girl he left behind, Annie Markham. But when he discovers his secret child—and that single mother Annie never stopped loving him—he's determined that a wedding will take place in the garden nurtured by faith and love.

Where healing flows...

Look for

The Wedding Garden
by Linda Goodnight

*Available May 2010
wherever you buy books.*

www.SteepleHill.com

Steeple
Hill®
LI87595

REQUEST YOUR FREE BOOKS!

2 FREE NOVELS PLUS 2 FREE GIFTS!

❖ HARLEQUIN®

Super Romance®

Exciting, emotional, unexpected!

YES! Please send me 2 FREE Harlequin® Superromance® novels and my 2 FREE gifts (gifts are worth about $10). After receiving them, if I don't wish to receive any more books, I can return the shipping statement marked "cancel." If I don't cancel, I will receive 6 brand-new novels every month and be billed just $4.69 per book in the U.S. or $5.24 per book in Canada. That's a saving of at least 15% off the cover price! It's quite a bargain! Shipping and handling is just 50¢ per book.* I understand that accepting the 2 free books and gifts places me under no obligation to buy anything. I can always return a shipment and cancel at any time. Even if I never buy another book from Harlequin, the two free books and gifts are mine to keep forever.

135/336 HDN E5P4

Name	(PLEASE PRINT)	
Address		Apt. #
City	State/Prov.	Zip/Postal Code

Signature (if under 18, a parent or guardian must sign)

Mail to the Harlequin Reader Service:
IN U.S.A.: P.O. Box 1867, Buffalo, NY 14240-1867
IN CANADA: P.O. Box 609, Fort Erie, Ontario L2A 5X3

Not valid for current subscribers to Harlequin Superromance books.

**Are you a current subscriber to Harlequin Superromance books
and want to receive the larger-print edition?
Call 1-800-873-8635 today!**

* Terms and prices subject to change without notice. Prices do not include applicable taxes. N.Y. residents add applicable sales tax. Canadian residents will be charged applicable provincial taxes and GST. Offer not valid in Quebec. This offer is limited to one order per household. All orders subject to approval. Credit or debit balances in a customer's account(s) may be offset by any other outstanding balance owed by or to the customer. Please allow 4 to 6 weeks for delivery. Offer available while quantities last.

Your Privacy: Harlequin Books is committed to protecting your privacy. Our Privacy Policy is available online at www.eHarlequin.com or upon request from the Reader Service. From time to time we make our lists of customers available to reputable third parties who may have a product or service of interest to you. If you would prefer we not share your name and address, please check here. ☐

Help us get it right—We strive for accurate, respectful and relevant communications. To clarify or modify your communication preferences, visit us at www.ReaderService.com/consumerchoice.

HSR10R

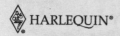
HARLEQUIN®

Showcase

On sale May 11, 2010

Reader favorites from the most talented voices in romance

Save $1.00 on the purchase of 1 or more Harlequin® Showcase books.

SAVE $1.00

on the purchase of 1 or more Harlequin® Showcase books.

Coupon expires Oct 31, 2010. Redeemable at participating retail outlets.
Limit one coupon per purchase. Valid in the U.S.A. and Canada only.

52609015

Canadian Retailers: Harlequin Enterprises Limited will pay the face value of this coupon plus 10.25¢ if submitted by customer for this product only. Any other use constitutes fraud. Coupon is nonassignable. Void if taxed, prohibited or restricted by law. Consumer must pay any government taxes. Void if copied. Nielsen Clearing House ("NCH") customers submit coupons and proof of sales to Harlequin Enterprises Limited, P.O. Box 3000, Saint John, NB E2L 4L3, Canada. Non-NCH retailer—for reimbursement submit coupons and proof of sales directly to Harlequin Enterprises Limited, Retail Marketing Department, 225 Duncan Mill Rd., Don Mills, ON M3B 3K9, Canada.

5 65373 00076 2   (8100)0 11651

U.S. Retailers: Harlequin Enterprises Limited will pay the face value of this coupon plus 8¢ if submitted by customer for this product only. Any other use constitutes fraud. Coupon is nonassignable. Void if taxed, prohibited or restricted by law. Consumer must pay any government taxes. Void if copied. For reimbursement submit coupons and proof of sales directly to Harlequin Enterprises Limited, P.O. Box 880478, El Paso, TX 88588-0478, U.S.A. Cash value 1/100 cents.

® and TM are trademarks owned and used by the trademark owner and/or its licensee.
© 2009 Harlequin Enterprises Limited

HSCCOUP0410

HARLEQUIN®

Super Romance®

COMING NEXT MONTH

Available May 11, 2010

HSRCNMBPA0410